DAFT WEE STORIES

LIMMY

LIBRARIES NI
WITHDRAWN FROM STOCK

D0280579

arrow books

9 10

Arrow Books
20 Vauxhall Bridge Road
London SW1V 2SA

Arrow Books is part of the Penguin Random House group of companies
whose addresses can be found at global.penguinrandomhouse.com.

Penguin
Random House
UK

Copyright © Brian Limond 2015

Brian Limond has asserted his right to be identified
as the author of this Work in accordance with the Copyright,
Designs and Patents Act 1988.

First published in Great Britain by Century in 2015

www.randomhouse.co.uk

A CIP catalogue record for this book
is available from the British Library.

ISBN 9781784750275

Printed and bound by Clays Ltd, Elcograf S.p.A.

MIX
Paper from
responsible sources
FSC
www.fsc.org
FSC® C018179

Penguin Random House is committed to a
sustainable future for our business, our readers
and our planet. This book is made from Forest
Stewardship Council® certified paper.

For everybody that can't be arsed with a real book.

CONTENTS

INTRODUCTION xiii

THE BITE 1

THE FAT WORKIE 7

THE FEMINIST 9

CLAUSTROPHOBIA 13

HAZY DAYS OF SUMMER 17

LUXURY APARTMENT 21

YOUR SHITE IS MY SHITE 23

THE BALL 29

HATE BEGETS HATE   41

FATHER OF THE BRIDE   43

HAPPY BIRTHDAY   47

THE RADIATOR   53

UPSIDE DOWN   61

DANCING   63

DESERT ISLAND   69

JINXED   73

STEVIE   79

THE FAKE   85

VEGETARIANS   89

NOTHING HAPPENS   93

DIRTY WEE SECRET   99

AN IDEA   107

THE BILL   113

THE JACKET   119

I HAVE SOME PICTURES   123

WHY I DON'T COME HERE   125

THE BREAK-IN   131

BEHIND THE TOILET WALL   135

THE WEREWOLF   141

ARNOLD'S ARSE   143

THE CONCERT   147

ARNOLD'S ARSE EYE   153

PUMP   157

CHEAT   163

THE BEAR COSTUME   165

FACEBOOK PAST   173

THE INFINITE TEA BAG   179

NAIL VARNISH   185

JANICE'S FACE   193

SEXUAL HEALTH CLINIC   197

WELCOME TO THE SHOW   205

WORKING IN A SUPERMARKET   209

THE TIP   215

MR NORMAL   221

THE GOAT   225

THE COUCH   227

I'LL LET YOU GO   231

ROOM WITHOUT A ROOF   235

THE MAGNET   239

THE TIGHT LACES   247

THE SIZE OF SALLY   251

A SIMPLE MISTAKE   257

BUTTERFLY   259

STREET LIGHTS	261
THE TEACUP	265
A VALUED MEMBER OF THE TEAM	271
THE CHIMNEY	275
THE BOWLING CLUB	283
THE GLOBE	287
ONE MAN HUNT	297
THE GAMBLER	303
SENSITIVE PETE	309
TOMATO SOUP	315
CRAP FILMS	319
THE WALLET	323
THE BLANK BUTTON	327
SMALL PRINT	331
ME AGAIN	335

THE PIGEON DANCE   339

LAPTOP   349

RENNIE   353

INTRODUCTION

Hello and welcome to my Daft Wee Stories. There are short ones, longer ones, thoughtful ones and stupid ones. Feel free to read them in order or just jump about to whatever ones take your fancy. It's your book, after all. And I hope you like it!

Limmy

THE BITE

'Fucking do it,' whispered Gary. 'C'mon. What are you waiting for? Do it!'

Things had been leading up to this for the past week. In a way, things had been leading up to this moment for years. A moment that would change his life for ever.

Last Thursday, Gary had shown his mates the picture he saw online. He found it after one of his usual late-night sessions of lying in bed with his phone, drifting from one site to the next, with no particular aim other than waiting to fall asleep. When he saw it, he sat up, and couldn't get his head down for hours. He couldn't remember what led him to it exactly. Fate, perhaps.

'And what?' asked one of his mates when Gary showed them what he'd found. It was an old 1800s sepia photo of a young man in his twenties, maybe his late teens, standing in front of a wagon. It was unremarkable by itself, but then Gary held up a finger to say 'Wait', then opened up Facebook. He typed in a name, which brought him to the page of Vincent, a nineteen-year-old he had working under him in the call centre. A pale sort of guy, skinny, with black hair; quite anti-social, and shite at his job. Gary clicked on Vincent's profile picture, then put it side by side with the photo of the guy from the past.

His mates burst out laughing. Because Vincent and this sepia guy were fucking identical.

'It's him!' shouted one of them. 'It's actually fucking him! Hahaha!'

'D'you think so?' asked Gary, completely serious. But nobody heard. They were too busy shouting out requests of what to search for on YouTube. A moment later, they were howling at a compilation video of dogs chasing their tails. All except Gary.

He stared through the video and thought more about Vincent and the guy in the picture. 'It's him,' his mate had said. 'It's actually fucking him!' Gary felt daft for asking his mate if he really thought so, not because it was a daft idea, but because it was daft to expect his mates to be open-minded enough to consider it. As open-minded as they were about everyday things like equality and who should be allowed to marry who, their minds were closed to certain other possibilities. Unlike himself.

Gary put that down to his insomnia. As he lay in bed each night, meandering online, he'd find himself gravitating towards sites that dealt with the strange and mysterious, the supernatural, the things that go bump in the night. They were the sorts of things that held no power over the imagination during the daytime, where they'd be laughed off or drowned out by noise. But there was something about the wee small hours that let unlikely ideas get their foot in the door. It was a time of night where you'd think 'What if?' And lying in the darkness, in silence, with no distractions, no urgent business, no conversations to move you away from that question, you were left facing it until it was answered. 'What if?' What if you lose your job and can't get another and you lose the house? Or what if you get that pain checked out and they tell you you've got six months to live?

Or what if the things that you don't believe in turn out to be real? What if there's a reason why certain things, certain beings, certain seemingly unbelievable beings, have cropped up in the stories of various cultures, thousands of miles and years apart? What if it's because they existed at one point? Or what if they still do exist, right in front of our noses, but we refuse to believe our eyes?

Gary thought about Vincent and the sepia guy. And when his mates were gone, he looked at the pictures and thought some more.

He spent the rest of the week thinking. Thinking about Vincent. Gary would watch him out the corner of his eye at work, looking for a sign that would snap him out of it, something that would slap him across the face and bring him to his senses, but it never came. His nights in the house were much the same, looking at the pictures of Vincent, past and present (he gave up thinking of them as two separate men). And he'd read stories, folklore and mythology, the myriad accounts down the ages that not only backed up his belief, but sickened him with envy. What must it be like?

And now he was alone with Vincent. Gary had asked to speak with him for a moment in the wee room where they kept the photocopier. They walked in, Vincent first, and Gary shut the door behind them.

'Fucking do it,' Gary whispered, pulling down the collar of his shirt, before turning his neck towards Vincent. For a second or two, Vincent did nothing, and a feeling of horror began to rise in Gary's chest. Would Vincent deny it? Would he call Gary mental and leave the office, before vanishing mysteriously without a trace? Or would he take Gary with him on a journey that would last a millennium?

'C'mon. What are you waiting for? Do it!' Gary felt like he was about to cry, until Vincent stepped towards him. Gary stepped back instinctively and bumped against the door behind him. He was aware that the door opened inwards, which would leave no room for it to open without him stepping towards Vincent. In other words, if Gary changed his mind and wanted out of there, he was fucked. But it was well past that point now.

Vincent clamped his mouth around Gary's neck, and began to suck.

Gary closed his eyes and felt like crying again, with joy. He thought of his mates, and how things would change. He wondered if he'd ever visit them, and show them what he'd become. He thought of his future, long after they were gone, and the many more mates that would come and go. The girlfriends, the wives. There would be sadness and loss, like in any form of lifetime, but he would experience love and friendship with his kind, his new kind, that would span centuries. He would travel far and wide, learn every language of every time. He would . . .

Gary realised that Vincent had stopped. He opened his eyes slowly, and looked upon Vincent's smiling face. It was done. No pain at all.

Gary looked around the room, to see the world for the first time through the eyes of the immortal. But there was no change. He looked out the window to the city below, bathed in the summer sunshine.

The sunshine! Oh my God, the sun! The sun!

But he hadn't burst into flames or turned into dust. Maybe that won't happen until tomorrow, he thought. Maybe it takes a day to kick in; Vincent would explain everything. He looked to Vincent, who was standing in a shaft of sunlight without so much as a blister. This didn't make sense.

Gary touched his neck and looked at his fingers. No blood. Maybe . . . no, this didn't make sense. He took out his phone and stuck on the front-facing camera to get a closer look at his neck.

A love bite. A big fucking purple bruise of a love bite about the size of a crisp.

They didn't speak much after that. Gary wore a scarf indoors for a couple of weeks. As for Vincent, he got a promotion, even though he was shite.

THE FAT WORKIE

There once was a fat workie. You've seen him before. High-vis jacket, helmet, steel-toe capped boots. And a belly like a space hopper.

He grafted all day, every day. You might find him lifting scaffolding poles out the back of a van, before carrying them halfway across the site, two at a time, to wherever they were to go. Or you might see him walking around with a wheelbarrow of building bricks, stacked high like a pyramid, as he shifted them from here to there. Or he might be taking an industrial-sized drill up to Mick on the third floor. Or pulling a thousand litres of water out of a hole, one bucket at a time. Or shovelling concrete for four hours straight.

Yet there he was with a belly like a space hopper.

He'd see the office workers, the men and women in suits, with their slim, toned bodies. He'd see them from the site, from a high point. He could see right in their windows, as they sat at their computers. They'd barely move a muscle, other than their fingers, to type. They'd sometimes move one of their hands to their mouse, to click a button, then move it back to the keyboard again. Sometimes they'd turn their neck a bit to look at somebody else, then move their mouth to speak. And that would be them, all day, every day, until it was time to leave. He'd see them walk to their motors and trains and buses, where they'd sit down again until it was time to get out, then walk a short distance to their houses, where they'd sit down in front of the telly for the rest of the night before lying flat in their beds for eight hours until it was time to get up and go to work and not move a muscle once again.

Yet there they were with their slim, toned bodies.

And there he was with a belly like a space hopper.

THE FEMINIST

There once was a guy who called a lassie 'one ugly bastard', right to her face. What d'you think of that then?

His name was Paul. What had happened was that there was this wee party – it was his mate's birthday – and there at the flat was the usual crowd, as well as the familiar faces of acquaintances that he sometimes saw at weddings. But there was the odd person he'd never met before, and he'd be introduced. On this occasion, he was introduced to the birthday boy's cousin and her husband. The first thing he noticed was that the husband was considerably better-looking than the wife, and he couldn't let that go without remark. 'I'll tell you something,' he said to her, in front of everybody within earshot, 'you've done pretty well for yourself, considering you're one ugly bastard.'

So, what d'you reckon? What d'you think of Paul? A bit cheeky, definitely, but what else would you say? Sexist?

Misogynistic? He didn't think so. Far from it. Paul thought he was brand new. A feminist, even.

He thought, well, if it had been the other way around, if it had been the husband that was the ugly one, he'd have said the exact same thing – to the husband, of course. It was a bit rude, but it was a funny thing to say, and something that most men laughed off. He'd seen it for himself. He'd seen the same sort of thing said to many men for as long as he could remember, right in front of the woman, and more often than not they'd both smile and nod in agreement. He'd even seen it on prime-time telly, on game shows, the type where they'd have a married couple on, like *Family Fortunes*. The host would say to the guy, 'Bloody 'eck, you're punching above your weight, ain't ya?' then everybody in the audience would have a right good laugh, as well as the millions at home, at just how unattractive the guy was.

So what was the difference in saying it to a woman? Why was saying it to the man all right, but saying it to the woman was bang out of order? If the host in one of these game shows said the same thing to the wife, well, it would be a career-ender, wouldn't it? But why? Paul's theory was thus.

All throughout history, men have imposed their values upon women using their physical strength. Back in the cavemen days, men would get what they wanted simply through force, no need to reason or explain. As things became more civilised, the use of force started to seem a tad lowbrow, with most men preferring to use words and intellect to put women in their place. If women disagreed, convincingly, by using their own words and intellect to greater effect, it was always understood that muscle would make the final decision, one way or another.

The power that men gained over women through brute force – or the threat of brute force – was then used to gain power over their minds, by excluding women from education, from voting, from many of the rights and expectations that men take for granted. After time, the values of heterosexual men, written by men, distributed by men, have become values for all people, both men and women alike. And with these men placing little value on a woman's intellect or self-determination, only one other aspect of the woman remains: her body. Her beauty. If there is no beauty, there is no worth.

And that, Paul thought, is what women have been taught to believe. After thousands of years, enduring scores of patriarchal cultures serving the base desires of heterosexual men, women have taught themselves to believe that their beauty is paramount. He knew that was wrong. He believed that men were able to laugh off criticism of their looks because deep down they knew they had so much more to offer. He felt that many women were unable to laugh off similar criticism because, deep down, whether they were aware of it or not, they had been programmed to believe that what they had to offer in compensation for any physical shortcomings was not as much as the male.

He simply couldn't go along with that. He felt that to

crack a joke about the looks of a man, but not of the woman, was to validate and perpetuate the inequality. And that is why he called her 'one ugly bastard'.

Anyway, she got her husband to put the prick in hospital.

CLAUSTROPHOBIA

There once was this lassie, Lesley, and she was boarding a flight to Australia, at long last. She couldn't believe this was happening. This was the plane she'd been dreaming about stepping onto for over five years now, ever since she first thought about emigrating. It started as a trivial remark about wanting to get away from Scotland, because of the weather. It's cold and wet, summer lasts a week, no wonder we're all alkies and junkies, it's fucking miserable – all that. And like anybody thinking about getting far away, she thought about the other side of the world. She was only thinking about a holiday at first, but as time went on, she started to dream bigger; she started to think about maybe spending a whole month there, or even travelling around for a year. Then she finally decided to fuck off for good.

She sat down and buckled up. It really was happening. As she watched the other passengers getting on, she could hear Australian accents all around. It made the dream more real, it made her feel like she was almost there already. But she'd have to wait a bit longer for the real thing itself. Just over twenty-two hours. Or just under twenty-four hours, if you want to look at it that way. Almost an entire day, sitting in one place. Christ, if she was stuck in the house for that long, she'd go off her nut.

Here, she thought. Imagine you wanted to get off. Imagine you started feeling pure claustrophobic and wanted to get off, but you couldn't. Imagine that.

She smiled, nervously. She wasn't claustrophobic, but she imagined what it would be like if she was. Wanting to get off but not being able to, like if she was in a submarine at the bottom of the ocean. That would be quite scary. No, she wasn't claustrophobic, but she was starting to feel scared of being claustrophobic. Claustrophobicphobic, haha.

These seats didn't give you a lot of room.

She took a deep breath and told herself not to be scared, and that surprised her. In fact, it scared her. It scared her that she was beginning to feel scared. That was something she could really do without, especially at the start of a twenty-four-hour flight. She was scared of being scared of being scared of being trapped in a plane for twenty-four hours with no way to get off. Claustrophobicphobicphobic, haha.

And that scared her. It scared her that she was beginning to lose track of what she was scared of. It scared her that she didn't know what happens when you can't take being that scared any more. It scared her that if she got in whatever state that was and people asked what was wrong, she wouldn't be able to tell them what it was she was scared of. Claustrophobicphobicpho . . . Fuck it, she got off.

She just got off. An air hostess asked her where she was going. 'I'm just . . .' was all Lesley said, and then she was gone.

I last saw her in Paisley. She was waiting outside a chemist, at eight in the morning.

It was pishing doon.

She looked freezing.

HAZY DAYS OF SUMMER

It was just one of those days. It was one of those crazy, hazy days of summer. Something about that heat just goes straight to your head, doesn't it? Puts your brain in holiday mode, makes you think that you're a thousand miles away without a care in the world. Aye, that's the best way I can put it. Your brain goes on holiday. It stops working!

That wouldn't have been a problem if I actually was on holiday with nothing to do, but as it turned out, I did have something to do. Well, not something I *had* to do, no way I was doing something I *had* to do on a beautiful day like that. It was something I *wanted* to do. Two things I wanted to do, to be precise.

The first thing I wanted to do was I wanted to thank the postman, for what he did. It was nothing, really. I'd been waiting for a parcel, recorded delivery, but I really fancied nipping over to the shops for a Solero. It's just one of those things I liked getting when the sun's out, I used to do the same thing with a can of Lilt, but I don't know if you get them any more. Anyway, the thing was that if I wasn't in to collect the parcel, well, it would get sent back to the depot and I'd have to walk there and back. Kind of defeats the purpose of getting something delivered, doesn't it? Plus I'd probably have had to search the house for my passport to show them at the depot. (And by the way, don't tell me you don't need a passport, a mate told me that once, but when I got to the depot they said that I did need it and I had to walk all the way back. I turned the house upside down looking for my passport, couldn't fucking find it. It was the last time I took that guy's advice, let me tell you.)

Anyway, that didn't matter, because of what the postman did. I nipped over to get a Solero, I just decided to go for it, I thought it'd only take a minute. But when I got there, I ended up getting caught up in this conversation with the guy behind the counter when I asked him if he had any Lilt. I don't even know if I wanted a can, I was just wondering if they still sold them. He didn't know what it was, so I was trying to describe it to him, it's harder than you think. (What does it taste like anyway, is it pineapple? I couldn't remember.) Anyway, I realised I'd been there for ten minutes or something, and I thought, Fuck! I nearly ran out without paying, then when I tried to pay, I dropped half my cash on the floor, I was all over the fucking place. That's what happens when you try to do something too fast some-times, like trying to get your jacket zip down or untying your laces, you just get in a muddle and it ends up taking you longer. I managed to pay him, then I sprinted out the door. I was 99 per cent sure I was too late. I thought, well, I'll make a run for it, but I was pretty sure I'd be taking that walk to the depot anyway.

But listen to this, guess what happened? The postman stopped me outside the shop! He had the parcel on him and he asked me if I wanted to just sign for it right there and then.

I think that is brilliant. I think that's the mark of a good postman who's good at his job, when he actually recognises the people he delivers to and does things like that. He didn't have to do that, he could have just taken it back to the depot; it was my fault after all, diving over for the Solero and going on about Lilt.

Before I got the chance to thank him, he was off. But there was no way I was letting that go without giving him a hefty pat on the back. I told myself that when I got up the road I was going to phone his work to thank him and tell him how much I thought he was doing a cracking job. And fingers crossed that his boss was listening in. You know, so he got brownie points or a wee pay rise or whatever. He deserved it.

So that was the first thing I wanted to do.

The other thing I wanted to do that day was that I wanted to kill the guy that murdered my da.

They said it was an accident, they said it wasn't murder, but it fucking was. When you show that degree of negligence, you prove yourself to have no respect for the safety of another man's life. And to me, that's murder.

But here's the funny thing. I got mixed up!

It's like what I said about it just being one of those days. You see, what was in the parcel was the thing I was going to use to kill Craig Malloy, the guy that murdered my da. (It was a trench knife, a kind of spiked knuckle duster with a knife coming out the side. You can get them online.) When I took it out the box, I think I must have got too excited, just wanting to get on with it. It's like what I was saying about trying to do something too fast, you just get in a muddle. A trench knife for Craig Malloy in a parcel from the postman. Parcel, Craig Malloy, trench knife, postman, know what I mean? And if you keep in mind the heat of that day, that heat that just goes straight to your head, it was no wonder what happened.

Before I had time to know what I was doing, I chased the postman up a tenement close and stabbed the utter fuck out of him on the stairs. Can't remember how many times, it was a blur. All I remember is him shouting at me saying that he didn't kill my da, but all I was thinking was, Aye, you would say that.

Then I headed back to the house and gave Craig Malloy a phone. I told him that I thought he was cracking. Told him that I thought what he did was considerate and thoughtful and, oh my God, I can't even tell you the rest, what an embarrassment. I can feel my face going red.

But you've got to laugh, man. You've got to. If you don't laugh, you'll cry. I'm shaking my head just thinking about it. But what can I say?

It was just one of those days.

LUXURY APARTMENT

They were going to put an offer in for the house. It was perfect, a terraced house on a leafy street, the type with trees coming out the pavement. Nice and quiet, but only a short walk away from the hubbub of the city, if they ever felt like getting in amongst it. It had three bedrooms, a living room at the front, and another living room type of thing at the back. Tons of space for both of them. He'd always fantasised about having a games room, and with all this he could have a games room and a home cinema. She quite fancied a gym. And they both loved the back garden, perfect for when they wanted to start a family, and perfect for getting mates round in the summer, for barbecues and that. And best of all, the price was right as well. It was fucking perfect.

Aye, they were going to put in an offer. Until they saw that poster on their way back home, the one outside that new development.

'Luxury apartments', it said.

Well, there was no point in having a look, the pair of them had already made up their minds about that terraced house, it was perfect. Mind you, the poster did say 'luxury'. They thought they'd better check it out. And two months later, they had the keys. To their luxury apartment.

No, it wasn't as big as the house, quite cramped in fact, but the estate agent said that meant it didn't take as much energy to heat. And no, it didn't have a garden, but then you don't have the pain in the arse of having to maintain one. And maybe it was in the middle of nowhere, but the noise from the neighbours through the walls made you feel like you were close to the hubbub.

And, aye, it cost about forty grand more than the house, way over their budget. Aye, it would probably postpone having children for a year or two. And aye, maybe their parents were right when all they could say was, 'It's a bit expensive for a one-bedroom flat.' But they were wrong about one thing.

It isn't a 'flat'.

It's an *apartment*.

A *luxury* apartment.

Just look at the poster: 'Luxury apartment'.

It says so right there.

YOUR SHITE IS MY SHITE

Hamish walked to the pub toilet and opened the door. A guy was leaving, so Hamish held the door open for him, and the guy walked past without a word of thanks. Oh, at your service, your majesty. Hamish walked into the toilet. A guy was at one of the sinks, washing his hands. He walked away from the sink, leaving the tap running, dried his hands with a paper towel, left the paper towel crumpled next to the sink, then walked out the door. Hamish shook his head, turned off the tap and put the paper towel in the bin. He didn't know why he bothered doing it, he didn't work there; maybe he just did it to annoy himself.

The toilet was empty now, except for him. He walked to one of the urinals, then decided to go to the cubicle instead. He only needed a pish, but he didn't want to have another encounter with these animals. He didn't want to pull down his zip and get started just for some guy to come in and join him, the pair of them pishing side by side, the other guy using the semi-private moment to get all his farts out. No.

So Hamish opened the cubicle door, walked inside, but then turned to walk right back out. It was fucking stinking. He had a look in the pan; the dickhead hadn't even bothered to flush, like it was so stinking that even the guy that caused it had to make a sharp exit. Shite was splattered everywhere like a shotgun blast. And, honestly, it was fucking stinking. And that, that smell, was everything that was wrong with people. That just summed it up for him. That smell, that putrid smell, was humanity.

People are disgusting, he thought. Fucking disgusting. Our disgusting ways ooze out of us like shite, both literally and metaphorically, to the disgust of whoever has the misfortune of being caught up in its presence. Oh, it wasn't just the guy at the door that didn't say thanks or the one who left the tap running and the litter, it wasn't just that. It was everything. It was just everything. The things we say, the things we do, the way we treat each other. The things you read in the paper that leave you wondering why. Why? Because we just can't help it, that's why, just as we can't help making the stench that comes out our arseholes. Vile creatures, so we are, pretending we're not, scrambling to disguise it, cover it up, waft it away, pretend it doesn't happen, or blame it on somebody else. And sometimes, as the case seemed to be in the literal shite here before him in the pan, we produce an odour so foul that not even we can bear to stay around long enough to flush the shite away.

Hamish wondered what the metaphorical equivalent of being disgusted by your own shite would be. He wasn't even sure if it was possible to do a shite so stinking that it disgusted even you yourself. He certainly couldn't remember such an occasion. It was an interesting thought.

Why, he wondered, are we all right with our own shites, yet everybody else's can get to fuck? Why was that? It's not as if other people's shites smell worse than our own, it's not as if our own shites smelled lovely. One shite was as bad as another, on average. This shite that he was currently being disgusted by, it could have been his own, theoretically. If an experiment was carried out where he was asked to do a shite in a toilet, before being administered with memory-erasing drugs, then brought back in to smell this shite that he was unaware was his own, he imagined he'd be just as disgusted by it as he was by this one in the pan right now. Conversely, if an experiment was carried out where he was brought into a toilet and told that the disgusting shite in the pan was his own, without being told that the shite was actually done by another guy, he could imagine that he'd think, Well, that's all right then, it's his own shite, it isn't disgusting any more – he'd maybe even stay in the cubicle a while to savour it. But the fact was this shite here, this one in the pan right now, was somebody else's shite, and that made it disgusting.

And he didn't like that. There was something about that way of thinking that he didn't like. He didn't like what it signified, not at all.

That way of thinking, now that he thought about it, that was everything that was wrong with people. That way of loving the smell of your own shite but hating the shite of others. Not just actual, literal shite, but that other shite, the symbolic shite, the metaphorical shite, the general shite within a person, the faults, the mistakes, the weaknesses, the shite that exists within each and every one of us. Had he himself always remembered to thank every person that ever opened a door for him, or remembered to turn off every fucking tap or put every fucking paper towel in every fucking bin? He didn't like the way we were disgusted by the shite of others but not so much by the shite of ourselves. Or, on a larger scale, the shite of our race, or the shite of our nation, or of our culture or religion or however else you want to look at it, our tribe.

Humanity, he concluded, as he looked into the pan, would never be as one until we could say that your shite is my shite. Until your shite is my shite. Why did Jesus not just say that? He could have just said that. The shite back then in biblical days was every bit as honking as the shite today, and would be for ever more. It's all Jesus had to say. It's all the Bible had to say. It's all God had to say.

Until your shite is my shite.

Until your shite is my shite.

He looked down at the shite in the pan. It was like somebody had put a firework in a jar of Nutella, it really was. He got down on his knees slowly, put his hands on either side of the toilet seat, closed his eyes and put his head inside the pan. Then he took a long, deep sniff of the excrement within.

He was sick. On the shite. And then he was sick again.

Which is a shame; I thought it was quite an interesting theory.

But don't ask me to go in there and try having a sniff myself – fuck that, man.

I don't even know the guy.

THE BALL

You've got a son, a wee boy, a wee three-year-old, and he loves playing with his football in the back garden. He loves throwing it more than he loves kicking it, he loves throwing it high in the air, as high as it can go, and watching it come back down. And sometimes he throws it so high it goes right over the fence, right into the neighbours' garden. You can't ask them to throw it back because they're never really out in their garden, and the fence is too high for you to quickly vault over and nab it. But it's all right, the following morning, it's back in your garden; they chucked it back. Your son starts throwing the ball about, as high as he can throw it, and oops, over it goes again. But the next morning, it's back. And then later in the day, you guessed it, over it goes once more. But it's all right, you know it'll be back the next morning, it always is. You get up, have breakfast, and your son asks to go out into the garden to play with his ball. You open the door and out the two of you go. He asks where his ball is. You look around and, well, no ball. Where's his ball? Is it still in the neighbours' garden?

You'd better go and have a peek.

You have a wee look through the gaps in your neighbour's fence to see if you can spot the ball. You look at the garden; you can't see it. You look to the right towards their house, you look left towards the back gate, but no, it's not there. Here, they've not just stuck it in the bin, have they? You almost couldn't blame them with the amount of times that ball's landed over there, but they wouldn't just stick it in the bin, would they? They fucking better not have. You know what you should do? You should go next door and ask them. Don't ask them if they put it in the bin, nothing confrontational like that, just ask them what they've done with it. See what they say.

So you nip next door and give their bell a ring. You don't like doing stuff like this but, you know, it's your son's ball. Your neighbour opens the door; it's the guy. He doesn't say hello, he waits for you to speak first, he's not a friendly sort. You ask him if he's seen your son's ball at all, knowing that he has. He tells you that they chucked it back last night, 'as usual'. You tell him that you can't see it, but he assures you they chucked it back last night, like they do 'every night'. He's hitting you with an attitude, basically. So you point out that that isn't true about him throwing it back 'every night', because your son doesn't throw it over every day, just

some days. Your neighbour shrugs it off and says that
they throw it back whenever, they don't know how often,
they've 'lost count', but they threw it back last night.
You're ready to reply to that 'lost count' bit, but he tells
you he has to go now, their dinner's in the oven, they
don't want it getting burnt. Then he shuts the door
without saying goodbye. What a fucking attitude, eh?

You go back to your garden, and you have another
glance about. No ball. No way they chucked that back.
Tell you what they did, they got sick of it landing in
their garden, so they binned it. You heard the attitude
on him when you went over, that thing about how they
chucked it back 'as usual' and having to chuck it back
'every night' when they don't. Total exaggeration. And
when he said that they've 'lost count'. Fuck off. Trying
to make you out to be a pain in the arse. No, trying to
make your son out to be a pain in the arse.

Your son looks around the garden and asks you where
the ball is. You tell him that your neighbours chucked
it back over but you don't know where it is. But that's
bullshit, isn't it? They didn't chuck it back. They
bullshitted you, and now they've got you bullshitting
your son. They're probably listening at their window,
probably having a right wee chuckle. So you correct
yourself and tell your son the truth, that you think that
lot next door put his ball in the bin. Your son asks why
they'd do that. You tell him that your next-door neighbours are naughty. Naughty. And you say 'naughty'
quite loud so that if the nosey bastards really are

listening at their window, well, they can get an earful of that.

A few days later, you're sunbathing in your back garden while your son plays about with a clothes peg. It should be a ball he's playing with, but he doesn't have one any more, so he has to make do with a clothes peg. Does that not make you fucking sick? It should, not just because he doesn't have a ball, but because now you can hear your next-door neighbours playing in their garden – playing with a ball.

A ball. And what's the bets it's the same ball, eh? What's the bets it's the same fucking ball?

You turn your head slightly to look through the gaps in the fence. Is it the same ball? Would they fucking dare? You can't quite see. But then you spot it as it flies high in the air for a moment, high above the fence. It's a football, but it's an actual football, whereas your son's football was more of a beach ball, to be fair. But that doesn't make everything all right. The fact remains that it's a ball. They're out playing with a ball while your son does without. Even if they didn't bin his ball, which they fucking did, it's the insensitivity of it. You've never seen them out with a ball before, not for a long time anyway, they're rarely out in their garden for anything, they were never there to chuck your son's ball back whenever it went over, and now they suddenly spring to fucking life with a ball when your son's ball goes missing? They're fucking rubbing it in, that's what they're doing. They're fucking rubbing it—

Their ball lands in your garden.

There's a wee silence. Your son looks at the ball, then looks at you. You can hear the wee lassie from next door tell her mum what happened. Then there's mumbling between the mum and the dad, maybe deciding on what to do. It must be a tricky one for them. After all, what do you do when your ball goes into the neighbour's garden a few days after you decided to bin theirs for landing in yours? It certainly is a dilemma. Do they seriously have the fucking cheek to ask for it back? Do they? The answer is aye, aye they do. The guy shouts over, sounding a lot more friendly than he was when you chapped on his door, now that he wants something. He asks you if you mind throwing back his daughter's ball.

Fuck that, man, pretend you're sleeping.

You shut your eyes, but you keep them open just enough to see what's going on. You can see the guy walking up to the fence. He asks again, a wee bit louder. You can hear his daughter ask why you're not throwing it back; it makes you feel a bit bad. But stay strong! Remember it was him that started this, not you. You can see him looking at you, before mumbling something to his daughter to say that you're sleeping. Fuck off, mate. Who does he think he is? Staring into your garden, telling his family what he sees; you should get up and tell him that's an invasion of privacy. But don't. Stay strong. You're supposed to be out for the count, just give it a few more seconds, he'll go away. You're doing well.

But now your son joins in.

He thinks it's a funny game, he's only three after all. He comes over to you, shouting, 'Wake up! Wake up! The ball. Give them the ball.' The poor wee guy wants you to wake up and throw the neighbours' ball back to them, even though he knows they're the same neighbours that put his own wee ball in the bin. It breaks your fucking heart. He starts shouting louder, to the point that it's going to be hard to keep up the pretence of sleeping for much longer. Fortunately, he stops, but unfortunately it's because he wants to pick up the ball and try throwing it over the fence himself. He can't do it, it's too heavy; this is an actual, real football we're talking. The guy next door puts his hands over the fence to help. His hands, over your fence, and into your fucking territory, fuck right off. That is trespass. If this was America, you'd be entitled to shoot him, shoot his fucking hands off anyway. But over here, you can't. It just isn't right. None of this is. Your son trying to throw a ball back to the guy who put his ball in the bin, it's just fucking wrong. Worst of all is that your son can't do it, and you're glad that he can't. This guy next door's got you pleased that your son isn't good enough while he spurs your son on and gives him encouragement. It's like he's turned your son against you and you against him. This guy's like the fucking devil, isn't he?

Then things go from bad to worse. Your son realises he needs to get a bit higher to throw the ball over, so he climbs up on the wee wall you've got running along the side of the garden. It's not a very high wall, it only comes up to your knee, but he could hurt himself. And he does. His foot slips away as he tries to lift himself up and his knee bangs against the edge. He starts to cry. He's not screaming, more like whimpering to himself, and looking over to you to make it all right. This is his fault, man, that guy, putting his hands over the fence, encouraging your son, it makes your fucking blood boil. You want to get up, but you can't, you're in too deep. They'll wonder how you can hear him crying all quietly at the other end of the garden yet you couldn't hear him shouting in your ear. They'll know you were pretending to be asleep and you'll look childish.

And now they're asking your son if he's all right. Mum, dad and daughter, all up at the fence, tending to your son with kind words, the people who stole his ball, making sure he feels loved and cared for while you do nothing, pretending to be asleep. Look what they've reduced you to. Just look at it. You are going to make these people pay. You have to. But for now, just lie there. Wait.

So you lie and wait, pretending to be dead to the world until they go back inside. Around two hours it takes. Two fucking hours. You stand up; your son tells you about his grazed knee and the ball in your garden. You ask about the grazed knee, but pretend to not hear the bit about the ball, in case they're up there listening. You go inside, make him some dinner, then put him to bed. You read him a book, but you don't put on your usual funny voices, you're not in the mood. Then you leave. And you wait until nightfall.

You wait until it's dark enough to go into your back garden without being seen by prying eyes, when you can get your hands on that ball. Their ball. And you won't be chucking it back over their fence, don't think that for a second. No, that ball is fucking getting it.

Go. Now. Pick up something sharp and go.

You pick up a pair of scissors lying on the kitchen worktop and you open the back door, and you walk up to the ball in your garden. Their fucking ball. Their stupid ball. And you stab it. You stab it three, four, five times.

More!

Six, seven, eight times.

Again!

Nine times. Until there's nothing left to stab, until you're poking at ribbons. Fucking hell, that felt good, didn't it?

Hold on, did you hear something there? Did you hear somebody in the neighbours' garden?

No. I don't think so.

You take the ball, or what's left of it, and walk towards the back gate; you're going to stick this fucking thing in the bin. You open the gate, find your bin and open the lid. But stop. Stop!

Don't put it in your bin. Put it in their bin. When they look through the garden fence tomorrow and see their ball's away, the first place they'll look is your bin. That's the way their minds work, takes one to know one and all that. So put the ball in theirs. Lift some of their bags up, stick it down deep, and put the bags back on top.

If they want their ball back, there it fucking is, mate, there it fucking is.

You turn around to find their bin.

And there's your neighbour.

He saw the lot. I think he saw the lot. I told you I heard something.

He asks you what the bloody hell you think you are doing. You try denying it, despite having a pair of scissors and a shredded ball in your hands. But I say it's too late to go on the back foot. Go on the offensive, that's what I say.

So you tell him he fucking started it by putting your son's ball in the bin. Too fucking right he did. Then it's your neighbour's turn to start denying it, saying he chucked the ball back over, he told you. Oh, he 'told you'. Know what to tell him? Tell him to fucking shut up.

You tell him, then he says he's going to phone the police and show them what you did to his daughter's ball. Aye, but first he'll need to get the ball, won't he? But you're not going to let that happen, are you? You try to disappear back into your garden with the evidence, but your neighbour follows you in and grabs at the ball. You push him away, because he shouldn't be in your garden, that's private property, that's trespass. Remember what you're allowed to do in America.

You stab him.

Not much, just a wee bit to get him to fuck off, no more than a scratch on his waist. But it's enough to make him think his life is in danger, and now he has to make a decision. Fight or flight? Fight or flight?

It's fight.

He goes for you, and what happens next is a mess. A bit of a mess. Hard to know who did what, it happened so quickly. Then it somehow came to an end.

And now you're lying out of breath in your garden with a gash on your cheek. As for your neighbour, you can see him through the gaps in the fence, crawling through his back garden to the safety of his house. Crawling like he's doing the sidestroke, with a pair of scissors in his chest.

It's not looking good.

You turn away and wonder. You wonder how this happened. You wonder how many years you'll get. And as you turn, you can see behind your garden shed. The space between the shed and the fence. Just a wee space. You didn't bother looking before. You didn't think anything would fit there. But there it is.

Your son's ball.

Oh dear.

Oh dear, look what you've done.

However did it come to this?

And now you're looking at me.

And I can see by the way you're looking at me that you think I should have known. I should have known the ball was there. Well, I didn't know. I'll admit, I thought I saw something when you were first looking, but I wasn't sure, so I didn't bother saying.

Anyway, that doesn't matter; the bottom line is that you did this. Aye, I might have pushed you a bit, but it was you that did it. If I asked you to jump in the Clyde, would you do it?

Right, I can see you're still looking at me that way, I'm sorry to see that. Sorry that you feel I was to blame. But I better go now.

It's my dinner.

My dinner's in the oven.

I don't want it getting burnt.

HATE BEGETS HATE

Hate begets hate.
Violence begets violence.
Chicken nuggets chicken.

FATHER OF THE BRIDE

The father of the bride stood up and tapped his champagne glass with a knife. Ding ding ding ding, smash.

He smashed the glass.

If it were you or I up there smashing that glass, the place would have erupted into laughter. Good-natured laughter. What a classic moment that would have been. But not this time. Nobody laughed. It wasn't because the father of the bride was a deeply serious man in particular. It wasn't because he had some kind of condition that led to him having accidents and nobody wanted to laugh at a guy that had something wrong with him, it wasn't that. The reason why nobody laughed was because the guy was an arsehole. How do I define an arsehole? Well, one example is that earlier that day he'd said something racist. And that's just one example. An arsehole.

He went to put the broken glass back down on the table, but it slipped out of his hand. He instinctively reached out to grab it, not thinking of the consequences of shooting your hand out towards a broken glass. He cut his hand open. A big gash down his palm and a few shards between his fingers. It was bad.

If it were you or I getting our hand slashed open like that, you'd have all these people running over to you, trying to help. You'd have somebody shouting for a bandage or maybe even an ambulance. You'd at least have a crowd around, offering their sympathy, asking if you're all right. But not this time. Nobody helped, because he was an arsehole. Earlier he'd patted the backside of one of the waitresses, in full view of the reception. There's another example for you. An arsehole.

He had to get a taxi to the hospital. Nobody would drive him, everybody said they'd had a drink, even the ones that were teetotal. It took half an hour before the taxi even showed, during which time he'd tried pulling out some of the shards of glass, cutting his hand open even more. When he finally got to the hospital and showed his hand to the triage nurse, it was much worse than when he first had the accident. Not a pretty sight.

Now, if it were you or I going to the hospital with our hand in that state, we'd get seen to right away, or if there were people with more serious injuries, they'd see to us as soon as they could. But not this time. They just kept telling him he'd be seen to any moment, which was a lie. He watched people come in after him with less urgent ailments, people who twisted their ankles or banged their heads, nothing where they were losing blood or needed to be stitched up quick – and yet they were being treated first. Any time he complained, he was told to just calm down and that he'd be seen to any moment. They kept telling him that for four hours until he decided to just leave. And good riddance to him. You see, he'd been in the month before. He'd started an argument in the waiting room about foreigners coming over here to use the NHS, plus he made a remark to a couple of nurses about how they were all wearing trousers these days and he'd like to see them back in skirts to give the men something to look at while they waited.

An arsehole.

Anyway, the reason I'm telling you this story is because I just saw him. Saw him about an hour ago. He was lying at the side of the road in his suit, just outside a J.D. Wetherspoon's. He looked like he's been dead for weeks.

If he was anybody else, back when he collapsed or whatever happened, I'm sure somebody would have asked him if he was all right. Somebody would have known that not everybody lying on the ground is drunk, they're perhaps diabetic or having a fit. And now, now that he is quite obviously dead, if it was anybody else, I would have phoned the council. I would have phoned the council or the police and made sure the guy's family was notified. If there wasn't any family, I would have organised the thing myself. I'd like to think so, anyway. I would have made sure the guy got a decent funeral, I'd have perhaps raised some money to give him a decent send-off, I would have tried to get some people to come along.

I'd probably visit his grave now and then to place some flowers there and give the gravestone a wipe.

But this guy? The father of the bride?

No.

He's an arsehole.

A known arsehole.

HAPPY BIRTHDAY

Chris sat in work on the computer, looking at a spread-sheet. He couldn't really get into it. It was his birthday.

He glanced at today's date at the bottom right of the screen. There it was. It usually gave him a wee rush of excitement seeing that date, like when he saw it last week on a carton of milk; Oh look, that's my birthday, he thought. He had no big cause to get excited, it wasn't like he had anything exciting planned, he was just going to come into work as usual. But, you know, you do expect things to be a wee bit different on your birthday, maybe a bit of extra friendliness from people, a bit of attention, that type of thing. But as the office worked away quietly behind him, it didn't look like that was going to happen. He thought that was a shame. Or maybe he was just being a big baby.

It's just, well, Chris could do with something like that, the friendliness, the attention. In here, specifically. Here in the office. People were a bit cold towards him, he felt.

It's not that they disliked him, they didn't want him out, they didn't put in complaints or anything, nothing like that. They just weren't as chatty with him as they were six months ago, when he started. It wasn't that the honeymoon period of being the new guy was over; there was another guy who had started around the same time and they were still chatty with him. The thing was, Chris wasn't very good at conversations. He never quite picked up the skill of knowing what to say and when, or knowing when to stop. He'd go off on tangents. He'd go quiet when asked a question, not realising a question had been asked. He'd say things that nobody would understand, like when he dropped in a reference to an obscure *Star Trek* character during a conversation his colleagues were having about a rug one of them bought in Ikea. And for that reason, people tended to give him a swerve.

So it was no wonder that they didn't know, or care, that today was his—

'Happy birthday to yooooou, happy birthday to yooooou!'

Chris turned around, wondering for a second whose birthday it was, surely this wasn't for him. But there they were, half the office walking over to his desk with a cake, with the other half looking over from their seats and smiling. Chris was smiling as well. He tried keeping tight-lipped to hide just how much it meant to him, but eventually he broke into a cheeser from ear to ear.

'It's very chocolatey, I hope you like chocolate,' said Janette the receptionist. Look at that. Janette barely spoke two words to Chris throughout the entire week, except to say good morning if she happened to be looking his way when he walked through the door. And here she was looking at him, carrying his birthday cake, having a laugh, like they were pals. Oh, he wasn't that sad, he knew they weren't really pals, but it was a nice feeling to go along with. It made a change.

'I do,' said Chris.

His colleagues laughed. All eyes were on Chris, and he liked it. For this brief moment, he was the most popular person in the company. It was just what he was after. A brief moment of experiencing the life of a well-liked person, a person that people like to be around. A brief moment of receiving unconditional good will. Just look at how they laughed when he said 'I do', despite it not being funny. What was so funny about that? Nothing. Yet they laughed. It reminded him of when he'd just started, when people would smile at him and give him their time, before they decided he wasn't worth it.

'Orange as well,' said Janette. 'It's sort of chocolate orange.'

'Mmm, nice,' said Chris, and they all chuckled.

There it was again. All he said was 'Mmm, nice', yet it was greeted with laughs and smiles. He'd seen them do it before with other birthdays in the office, it was like a short burst of condensed niceness. Maybe it was done to save time so that they wouldn't have to be nice all day, which could interfere with work, or maybe people were temporarily intoxicated with the excitement of the event. He didn't want it to end, but he knew it wouldn't last. It'd only be a matter of minutes before the laughing and smiling was done and everything went back to normal. Less than a minute, even. If only he could have even a fraction of this, day to day, just a fraction. But no. Back to normal. Back to dodging him, and leaving group conversations one by one, and neglecting to mention that they're going for a drink. Until this time next year. God, why did he have to talk so much shite, what was wrong with him?

But could this not be a second chance? A way to wipe the slate clean? Could he not use this opportunity to reconnect with everybody? Instead of them leaving the kitchen when he walked in, they'd maybe hang about a bit for the birthday boy, and he'd try his hardest not to go on so much or say things that nobody had a clue about. His hopes of ever striking up a friendship in here seemed dead in the water, but maybe this short burst of niceness he was receiving would be like a shock to the heart, bringing his hopes back to life. You never know, this time tomorrow they could be saying, 'That Chris is all right, when you get to know him.'

He looked at them again, realising he'd tuned out, but they were still smiling. It was wonderful. This is what it felt like when people hung on your every word, and that is exactly how it felt. It really was like they were hanging there, going nowhere, with nothing to do other than hear what he had to say next. And whatever he said, they would laugh. They would laugh no matter what. He really could say the first thing that came into his mind, and they'd laugh.

So he did.

'Shower curtain,' he said.

He waited for the laughter. It didn't come.

'Shower curtain,' he said once more.

It was a long time until his next birthday. It was only a year, of course, but it felt longer. Much, much longer.

THE RADIATOR

The house was freezing, despite Des having the heating up full-blast. He had the boiler right up to ten, the most it would go, and the same went for the knobs on the radiators. But the radiators just didn't seem to be making a dent. They were warm, but that was about it. They weren't like his mate Benny's radiators, you could iron your clothes on them, they were roasting. But these? These were fucking useless. He wondered if it was because the knobs on his radiators only went up to five. That was the most they would go, but maybe that was why they only felt half as hot as Benny's, because half of ten is five. He didn't know, so he gave Benny a phone.

Benny told Des that it doesn't make any difference what the numbers are on the knobs, as long as they're up to the max. 'You stupid bastard,' said Benny, in a nice way. But Benny did have one idea about what might be the problem. He asked Des to tell him if the radiators were as cold down the bottom as they were up the top.

Des asked what he was on about; Benny told him to just do it. So Des pressed his hand against the bottom of the hall radiator, and yelped. It was hot as fuck. Des asked Benny what the story was there, and Benny told him that his radiators needed to be bled.

'They need to be what?'

Benny sighed, and explained what needed to be done. All Des had to do was unscrew the wee thing at the top left of the radiator, and that would let out all the excess air. That's why the hot water wasn't getting up to the top, there was a big air bubble inside. Des asked Benny how it got there, but Benny told him it was late and he was tired and he really didn't want to get into all that. He just told Des to unscrew that thing and let out the air, but make sure there was a pot handy, because at some point all the air would be out, then you'd get water skooshing out the hole. When that happens, turn the wee screw tight again, and that'll be it done. The radiator will be boiling hot, from top to toe. Easy. Easy as pie.

'Could you come round and do it?' asked Des.

'No, mate,' said Benny, and hung up.

So Des got on with it himself. He had a look for the wee screw thing on the radiator in the living room, and sure enough, there it was. He had a look at what type of screw hole shape it had, and it was the type he could just use a knife with, which was just as well, because he didn't have a screwdriver. He went into the kitchen, got a pot out of the cupboard, then went to the drawer to get a knife. Then he brought the knife through to the living room to give this thing a shot.

He slid the knife into the hole of the wee screw and started to turn it. It didn't budge. He tried harder, closing his eyes slightly in case the end of the knife broke and pinged into his eye, but it still didn't budge. Then he remembered that he probably needed to turn it the other way, because he was unscrewing, not screwing. He was right, because when he did it, out came that air that Benny was talking about. It sounded good. It felt good as well, like letting down somebody's tyre. Tssssss. God, he used to do that all the time, him and Benny, back in school. Some laugh, that. If a teacher gave one of them lines, then they'd go to the car park and—

Des felt warm water skoosh onto his forearm, giving him enough of a fright to drop the knife. He saw the manky radiator water land all over the white carpet, and he panicked. He couldn't make up his mind about whether he should reach for the knife to screw the thing tight, or reach for the pot to catch the water. He decided to go for the pot, then realised that he had forgotten to bring the fucking thing through from the kitchen. But then rather than just quickly grabbing the knife and tightening the wee screw like anybody else would, he ran away to the kitchen to grab the pot. Then, when he was only about two paces away from the pot, he realised he should have just grabbed the knife, and he doubled back. And when he got to the living room, he couldn't find the knife, even though it was right fucking there in front of him. He was flapping. The white carpet was being ruined, his landlord would take it out his deposit, and it would probably drip down to the neighbour below. Add that to everything else he'd fucked up, and he was definitely getting booted out the building, unless he did something and did it fast. He didn't know what to do, so he did the first thing that came to mind.

He started drinking the water.

He could have just held it in his mouth to buy him enough time to find the knife and screw the wee thing tight then run to the kitchen and spit it out and brush his teeth and all the rest of it, but the thought never occurred to him. Instead, he just lapped it up frantically like a thirsty dog drinking out a tap. His hands scrambled around underneath, out of vision, and eventually found the knife. He began screwing the wee thing, but it made no difference. He'd broken it! There's no way he'd be able to keep drinking, the water from the entire central heating thing would flood downstairs and . . . then he realised he was screwing it the wrong way. He screwed it clockwise, the water stopped, and he fell back onto the floor, exhausted.

Des, Des, Des. You silly, silly man.

He lay there for a minute, wondering about how he was going to get the stain out of the carpet. It also dawned on him that he could have just held the water in his mouth instead of drinking it. But it was too late now. He drank it, and it was fucking minging.

But.

Wait a minute.

Wait.

It wasn't minging.

It felt minging, aye, and it probably looked minging, drinking water from a radiator. But did it taste minging, Des? Did it?

No, it didn't. In fact, as he licked his lips and swirled his tongue around his mouth, he concluded that it was far from minging.

It was delicious.

Really delicious.

It was perhaps the most delicious thing he had ever tasted. Des couldn't believe it. Wait till he told Benny about this! Des picked up his phone, but then thought against it. What if he was talking shite? Like, it might not be the manky radiator water that was delicious, maybe it was some delicious food he ate earlier that was trapped between his gum and cheek and the radiator water dislodged it. But it couldn't have been that, because all he'd had to eat that day was baked beans and a pear. Or maybe the manky radiator water was tasty because he'd just brushed his teeth, and sometimes when you brush your teeth then taste something, it tastes different. But he hadn't just brushed his teeth; that was a stupid thing to think. Or maybe it was just the whole stressful situation that had just happened, and it was all in his mind, because sometimes stress like that can make people see things that aren't really there or hear things that aren't being said, or taste delicious things that are in fact manky. Well, he'd calmed down now, so he thought he should just taste the thing one more time to draw a line under it.

He picked up the knife, put his mouth to the wee hole thing on the radiator, and unscrewed. A jet of manky radiator water sprayed into his mouth. That's all he wanted, just a sip, and he quickly screwed the thing tight again. He swished the liquid around inside his mouth, then gulped.

Fucking hell, man, it was more delicious than before. He'd never tasted anything like it. He tried comparing it in his head to his favourite drinks, his favourite booze, his favourite juice, but they all seemed like pish water compared to this stuff. Yet it seemed more than just a drink. It was like a meal, it was like a main course and a dessert, stuff that shouldn't go together, but it did; it was like something out of *Willy Wonka*. He didn't think it was possible for anything to be this tasty. He'd seen programmes about top-notch restaurants where it costs you a bomb to get this wee plate of food, and he couldn't comprehend something being that tasty that it justified skinning yourself that much. But this stuff in his radiators, fuck, he could imagine people selling their house for just another swig.

Des picked up his phone again to tell Benny. Who knew where this was going?

'Benny, you've got to get round here,' he said, but before Benny even had a chance to reply, Des hung up. He just wanted one more taste. He just wanted to be sure, that's all. He didn't want to make a tit of himself, as usual. So he'd have one more taste. He wondered if it would be even tastier the next time. And the time after that. But for now he'd have just one sip, that's all. Just one. Just one more.

Benny phoned back to see why Des was phoning, but it just rang out. It was probably nothing, but he didn't like the sound of that. What was it he said? 'Benny, you've got to get round here.' He tried phoning again; it rang out. He left a message; nothing back. He sent a text, then another. Nothing. He was going to leave it, Des had probably just flooded the place, it could wait till tomorrow. But what if it couldn't? What if Des was in trouble, and he had to live with that for the rest of his life? He needed a bit of perspective here, so he phoned Des's dad to get a second opinion. Des's dad reminded Benny that anything was possible when it came to Des, and Benny agreed. So they got round there as quick as they fucking could.

The pair of them rang the bell and banged the door, shouting for Des to open up. There was no answer, so Benny knew what had to be done. He told Des's dad to get out the way, before taking a runny up to the door and battering the thing open with his shoulder. They raced into the hall, with Des's dad heading to the living room and Benny sprinting off to the kitchen. When Benny heard Des's dad wailing, he knew that Des had been found. Benny ran into the living room, and there he saw it.

Des was lying conked out next to the radiator, his face wet with some kind of murky brown liquid around his mouth, and he'd urinated himself. Des's dad was in bits.

That was six months ago. And since then, a lot has changed. Des has changed. When he got out of hospital, the first thing he did was to get counselling. It wasn't something he was talked into by his dad or by Benny, it was his own decision, and he attends meetings almost every day. He got up himself to talk at one last week, to inspire and warn others. His dad and Benny were there to lend their support. He said that even to this day, six months on, he still can't be sure if the manky radiator water really was as delicious as he thought it was, or if it was indeed only in his imagination due to stress. But one thing was for sure, he wasn't going to find out. If he hadn't got his stomach pumped that night, that would have been him, kaput. He wasn't going back there just to satisfy his curiosity, and he urged others to do the same.

And then he said something. Something that I hope you will take with you. A word of advice.

He said that if you are thinking of bleeding a radiator, it is vital – absolutely vital – that you have a pot ready. 'I cannot stress that enough,' he said.

And when he said that, Benny nodded.

UPSIDE DOWN

Well would you look at this, everything's upside down. No, it isn't a mistake. I asked the folk that make the books if they could do this sort of thing and they said yes. I didn't really think I would go ahead with it, but here we are.

I wonder what you look like right now, holding a book upside down. I wonder if anybody can see you. If you're reading this on some kind of e-reader thing, I don't think anybody will notice, but if this is an actual book and somebody sees the cover upside down, they'll be wondering what the score is with you.

If you're reading this in the house and somebody walks in on you, you'll look like you've been up to something and you quickly grabbed the book when you heard footsteps. If they ask you what you're doing, you could show them the upside-down page, but they might not ask. They might just come to their own conclusions and say nothing. That sort of thing makes people drift apart.

Or maybe you're a guy reading this on a beach. A guy on the beach holding an upside-down book. You'll look like a perv. You'll look like you're pretending to be trans-fixed on an interesting story, when in fact you're transfixed on somebody's arse. Or a child.

Or if you're on a bus or train, you might look suspi-cious, trying to appear to be normal. But you're not – your book's upside down, your mind's on other matters. A bomb, perhaps? Look around: is anybody looking at you with suspicion? Oh dear, you looked around, now you've gone and made yourself look all shifty. Anyway, I thought I'd try this out, maybe get you into a spot of bother for a laugh.

I hope you're not dead.

DANCING

Jamie staggered away from the club; he was an absolute disaster, zigzagging from one side of the pavement to the other. He wasn't quite sure if this was the right way home. He wasn't quite sure if home is where he wanted to head. Was he not heading for a taxi? He couldn't remember. Maybe the bus. But where was his money, where was his wallet? Was it in his jacket? But where was his jacket? Did he leave it in the cloakroom? Did he even come out with a jacket tonight? He just couldn't remember, he just didn't know. His head was wasted, his brain felt like it had been bounced about in a tumble dryer for three hours. He just didn't know. He did know one thing, though: this was his last night of dancing. It was no longer for him. And that was a big deal.

It was a big deal because dancing was something he looked forward to all week, every week. It was one of the few things that made Monday morning bearable, knowing that he was only four days away from Friday night and whatever club he'd end up in. Around Wednesday, he and his mates would start chatting online about where they planned to go. Depending on the line-up over the weekend, they'd maybe decide to take it easy on the Friday and save themselves for the Saturday, or vice versa. Sometimes they'd go daft on the Friday and even dafter on the Saturday. And on the rare occasion, they'd go a wee bit daft on the Sunday night as well. To mix things up, they'd sometimes take a drive up north or down south for a change of scenery, or just stay local but visit two or three clubs in one night. And, of course, there were the dance festivals, there was Ibiza. He blew a fortune on it all, and it was worth every penny.

Tonight was his favourite time to go clubbing: the last Saturday of the month here in Glasgow. It was one of the big Saturdays where Jamie and his mates had taken it easy the night before, so when they all met up in the pre-club pub, everybody was tip-top and full of life, no heavy comedowns or hangovers, nothing that couldn't be sorted with a drink or two, at least. To Jamie, this was what it was all about, catching up with everybody, tapping his feet, bobbing his head, handing over his cash to whoever got the pills this time around, then clinking glasses with a wink and a smile. Eventually they headed round to the club, where the bass from the inside filtered through to the queue, before booming their chests as they walked through the door.

That was when the night began, as far as Jamie was

concerned. As much as he loved the chatting and drinking that came before, he was here for the dancing. All around were people at various stages of their night out. Some, like Jamie, were just standing around on the outskirts, patting their legs with their hands as they drank their drinks, waiting for their pills to kick in. Others were in full swing – hands in the air, not giving a fuck – and it didn't take long for Jamie to join them. He and his mates would stick together for a while, moving from one room to the next, following their ears, before breaking off into wee groups, then wee-er, until Jamie was left dancing by himself.

He looked forward to that the most. Dancing alone, surrounded by a sea of strangers. He could lose himself in that. With mates by your side, you sometimes felt the need to check up on them and ask them how they were doing or what they thought of the tunes, and they sometimes felt obliged to do the same. But when you're there by yourself, you can wander here and there without having to tell somebody where you're going. You can dance in new and unusual ways you've never danced before, without your mates looking you up and down. You can go into your own wee world, floating from one strange thought to another, without interruption.

And it was then, just after two in the morning, that he had one of these strange, funny thoughts. It stopped him right there, in the middle of the dancefloor, as the rest of the club danced around him.

What are we doing? he thought.

He looked to the clubbers in front of him, the ones closer to the DJ, and watched them from behind as their shoulders and arses boogied away. A smile crept across his face. Then he glanced to the people to his side, and watched their faces as they moved in time to the music, here, in a darkened room full of people they don't know – the fact that some of them looked deadly serious made him smile even more. Then he turned around to look at the rest of the club behind him. He saw one lassie reaching her hands out to random locations on each beat, like she was one of those 1950s telephone exchange operators, pulling out invisible cables and putting them back in. There was an angry-looking guy with his top off who looked like he was marching on the spot while knitting. And there was a lassie with her eyes shut, shaking her head and wagging her fingers side to side, like she was telling a wee boy that her answer was no and she won't hear another word about it.

He had to bite his bottom lip to stop himself from laughing. Honestly, he thought. 'What the fuck is this?'

The crowd cheered at some bit in the song, and he started to dance again. Until he realised what he was doing. He realised he didn't know what he was doing. He looked at himself moving his arms and legs about, next to other people doing the same. It felt fucking mental. This whole thing suddenly felt like the most mental thing in the world. It felt peculiar. He tried one more time to start dancing and get back into it, but when he saw his hands wave around in front of his face, he thought, What are you fucking doing, mate? and stopped.

He shook his head and smiled, then turned to his mates to tell them about it, this thing that had popped into his mind, but then he remembered they weren't there. Just as well, really, it could have ruined their night. He could imagine how it would go. He'd tell one of them, then they'd be unable to dance, just like him. Then his other mates would ask why neither of them were dancing, which would pass it on to them, like a virus. It'd only be a matter of time before the other clubbers asked why a group of a dozen people were standing in the middle of the dancefloor, static. And then one by one, they'd all stop dancing as well, every last one of them.

Jamie laughed at the thought. A whole club not dancing. That's the sort of thing that could get a place shut down. A whole club not dancing, then walking out, then tweeting about it on their way home. Other clubbers in other clubs would read about it, catch the bug, stop dancing and fuck off up the road as well, never to return. Forget about all this other shite that can ruin a club like drug busts and fights, there's an idea that could crush the entire clubbing scene in a fucking weekend. For ever.

He turned to the guy next to him, some sweaty guy dancing with an empty bottle of water. Jamie just had to get this one out.

'What are we doing, eh?' shouted Jamie over the music.

'What's that, mate?' asked the guy.

'I said—'

A fist came flying into the back of Jamie's head from nowhere.

The bouncer dragged him by the hair to the door, punched him once more in the chops and literally kicked his arse out onto the pavement. When Jamie looked up to the bouncer for an idea of what the fuck just happened, he got another boot in the arse, and one in the head for good measure.

Jamie wasn't the only one to have had that zany thought, you see. The bouncer, having stood rooted to the spot in club after club for over twenty years, had thought the very same thing, many, many times.

It kept him awake at night, so it did. The impact that would have on the business. A lot of good lads in security would lose their jobs, many of them with families to feed and bills to pay. So when he overheard that loud-mouth on the dancefloor, the one that had stopped dancing, well, I'm sure you'll understand . . .

You've just got to nip that sort of shite in the bud.

DESERT ISLAND

He was on an island. Somewhere. He didn't know. The Pacific, maybe. The type he used to see in picture frames, hanging up in offices and waiting rooms, to help take people's mind off things. The type you'd see pictured from above, green in the middle, within a ring of white sand, surrounded by an ocean of blue. He'd sometimes look at pictures like those if life wasn't going that well, wishing he could be on that island, wherever it was, far away from everybody that was doing his nut in. And now here he was, on one, with palm trees to his left and a sunset to his right, watching his bare feet sink into the soft, powdery sand as he walked along the beach, slowly, like a man with all the time in the world.

Hell. Hell on earth.

It was the loneliness. James had been stuck on the island for over two years now. Maybe three. Or maybe five, it was hard to say. He didn't keep track, not to begin with anyway. Keeping track was for people who wanted to count the days until they were rescued, like the castaways you'd see in films. It helped prevent them from losing the plot. But he didn't want to be rescued; this was like a dream come true. If anybody had tried to rescue him back then, he'd have climbed up one of those palm trees and told them to fuck off.

But that was then. After a while, one day of sand and sea began to merge into every other day of sand and sea. Sand and sea on a Saturday. Sand and sea on a Tuesday. He'd fall asleep looking at it all, and when he'd wake up, there it would be, same as before. He found himself counting ants under a rock one day just to give himself something to do, and that's when he knew it was time to start counting days instead. Then he just counted weeks. Or was it months? He couldn't tell you how long he'd been there, he really couldn't. Could have been five hundred years, for all he knew. Nobody told him otherwise, because since arriving on the island, he hadn't spoken a word to another living soul.

And that was killing him. The loneliness. If anything on this island would finish him, it was that. He didn't know why he cared so much, maybe it was because everything else was taken care of. He didn't have to worry about food or drink: there was plenty, not only from the island but also from everything washed up in the wreckage. And he wasn't worried about being eaten himself, nothing here was capable of that. A wild boar, maybe, if it had a go at his face while he slept, but he doubted it – they seemed as scared of him as he was of them. No, he wasn't worried about boars or going hungry. That wasn't what killed you in a place like this.

It was the loneliness. The never-ending loneliness.

Yet as he looked up from his feet to the beach in the distance, he saw something that told him that maybe he wasn't alone after all. Something on the sand. Walking. He rubbed his eyes, and looked again.

It was a man.

It couldn't be, could it? James searched for alternative explanations for the sight. He didn't want to get his hopes up, only to get closer and discover that it was merely a man-shaped tree stump. In his fragile state of mind, an upset like that might put him over the edge. He might go berserk and start punching fuck out it, causing himself an injury. Or worse, he might decide to befriend it.

But after a few more paces, he could see that there would be no need to brace himself for an upset. It was a man, definitely a man, with ragged trousers and a beard coming down to his belly. And he was walking this way. James began wondering who the man was, how he got here and when. But as they drew closer, James knew that the man had arrived here the same way as himself. He recognised him. He remembered him vaguely from the cruise.

The cruise! Jesus, he'd almost forgotten. It seemed like centuries ago. Now, seeing this guy, it was all coming back.

The cruise. It was his wife Lisa's idea. They'd never been on a cruise before, it was never something he fancied, but they saw it on a shopping channel on a particularly shite telly night. What started off as a slagging session of the presenter turned into them both saying, 'You know, that actually looks quite nice.' There were videos showing people relaxing on deckchairs around the swimming pool, there was an all-inclusive bar, and the food looked good. It looked all right. A nice, lazy way to spend a fortnight. The reality, of course, was a bit different.

The deck chairs by the pool were nabbed each morning by the same dozen or so couples, who would get up at the crack of dawn to claim the chairs with their towels, then bugger off for half the day. The all-inclusive bar was at least three people deep from midday onwards; you didn't stand a chance of being served unless you were a queue-jumping prick who didn't give a fuck. As for the food, the food was nice, but not where you had to eat it. Your table was numbered, and there you would eat in front of the exact same people three times a day for two weeks solid, getting to know the sights and sounds of each other's eating habits intimately.

By the end, nobody liked anybody. Nobody even tried to pretend. Yes, it was all coming back to him now. And as the guy brushed past James without saying a word, James breathed a sigh of relief.

He reckoned it had all come back to him, too.

JINXED

'What are we doing here?' asked Claire, as Marty drove them into the scrapyard. It was a Friday night. They were supposed to be going for a meal.

'Oh, I forgot to tell you. I'm thinking of getting a new motor.'

She looked at him. 'That's good, Marty. But . . .'

'I know this isn't the best time,' he said, 'but I wanted to nip in before they shut for the weekend; just want to find out what they'd give me for this.'

'All right,' she said, shrugging and shaking her head.

That was very diplomatic of her, considering. She was starving. He'd told her he was taking her out for a meal, so she made sure she didn't have that much for lunch and she kept away from the snacks. Now she was starving. Done up to the nines on a Friday night, starving, in a scrapyard.

Any other couple would be arguing like fuck at this, but they were loved up to the eyeballs. They'd been seeing each other for five years, but it was like they had only just started going out – it was still fresh and fun and surprising. That was mainly down to Marty, and the fact he was a bit of a dafty. The things he'd do, the things he'd say. It was like he just didn't have a clue, about anything. She found that out quite early on, when they first went to see a film together, with him leaning over every minute to ask who was who and why was this and how come they were doing that. He was just so fucking stupid, it used to do her nut in. But eventually it was one of the main things that kept them going through thick and thin, because the pair of them would have such a good laugh together, mainly at Marty's expense. And no wonder. The amount of shite that went over that guy's head, it was hysterical.

Marty got out the motor and walked over to some guy in a hard hat at the wee portacabin office in the distance. Claire watched in the rear-view mirror as Marty said hello to the guy, before doing that same thing that Marty always did at the start of any conversation with a stranger. He just stood there saying nothing, trying to find the right words to say before saying them, his mouth open, his eyes looking up and to the right, like a schoolboy that had just been asked to do some hard-as-fuck sum in his head. He never used to do that, but Claire had taken the piss out of him so much over the years for the things he'd say. The howlers he would come away with in front of the telly, the questions he'd ask, the comments he'd make, the stuff that revealed that he just didn't get it. Claire would turn her head towards him and say, 'Tell me you're joking,' but there he'd be with his face all red. So these days he just learned to keep it zipped until he had a wee think beforehand. Or sometimes he just kept his thoughts to himself.

Marty eventually started explaining whatever it was he was trying to explain to the guy in the hard hat. The guy looked at his watch, nodded, then turned to walk away. Marty reached out his hand for a handshake, but the guy didn't see, so Marty pretended that he was actually putting his hand out to then bring it up to his face for a wee scratch of his chin. Claire laughed. Nice try, she thought. He was such a clown, he really was. He was like Stan Laurel or something.

The scrapyard claw crashed through the roof, taking off her left arm and a few of her ribs. For a split second, she wasn't sure what had just happened. She glanced at Marty through the rear-view mirror, as if he'd be able to shed some light on the situation, but he looked like he didn't know what was happening either. His hands were on his face and he was screaming, like that guy from that painting, she couldn't remember its name right now.

The claw's grip began to tighten, crushing the sides of the motor and her along with it. Her organs were squeezed out the hole where her arm used to be, like a tube of three-stripe toothpaste. Marty looked on, frozen to the spot, as the claw lifted the motor towards the crusher. He turned to shout at the guy in the crane, but nothing came out. Nothing. And he stayed like that, speechless, as the motor was dropped into the big machine that squashed his vehicle and girlfriend into a one-metre cube of metal, plastic and sludge.

'Claire! Oh my God, Claire!' he shouted, finally finding his voice. The guy in the hard hat ran from the crane; he didn't know what the fuck was going on, but he soon worked it out. Him and Marty ran over to the bleeding block of steel.

'Claire,' said Marty quietly. He didn't know what to do. What was he to do now?

He turned to the guy in the hard hat, slowly.

And smiled.

The hard-hat guy started getting worried. Very worried.

But it was all right!

Because what the crane guy didn't know was there was this programme called *Jinxed*. It was a hidden-camera show, a bit like *Candid Camera* or *Beadle's About* or *Punk'd*. They'd do a big practical joke, then the film crew would appear at the end, along with the presenter who'd say, 'You've been jinxed!'

Claire and Marty had watched it the other night. It was another one that Marty didn't quite get. He just wasn't sure about one or two things. Pretty fundamental things, as it turned out. He was going to ask Claire at the time, but he didn't want her to take the piss again. Anyway, he reckoned he got the gist of it and how it all worked.

The guy in the hard hat ran away to phone an ambulance. And the police. Marty glanced around for the film crew. They were nowhere to be seen.

'You've been jinxed!' shouted Marty.

But still no film crew appeared. And where was Claire? He hoped this didn't take too long. They were supposed to be going for a meal.

Daft Marty.

The amount of shite that went over his head.

It was hysterical.

STEVIE

I'm in a shop. An electrical shop. The kind that sells tellies and cameras and things for your computer, that kind of place. And I'm at the counter being served. I won't bother telling you what I'm buying, you wouldn't be interested. I'm not even interested. You buy stuff, hoping it'll make you happier, but it never really does. Well, it does a wee bit, but not as much as you were hoping for.

Anyway, I get served by the guy. Looks about twenty-eight. And his wee name badge tells me his name is Stevie.

'All right? Let me take that for you, mate,' says Stevie, and gives me a smile and a wink.

That did something, that. What he did there, that smile and a wink. I don't know what it was exactly, but that did something. It wasn't a big, giant smile. It wasn't a big fake Disneyland smile where we're all pretending we've worked everything out and nobody dies any more. It was just a wee smile, that kind of smile where you keep your mouth shut and tense up your cheeks. Friendly, but considerate. Considerate of my feelings. He thought I'd maybe want a smile, but he was considerate enough to not ram his joy down my throat with a cheesy Cheshire-Cat grin.

Then there was the wink. In case the smile seemed too reserved, the wink made up for it. But it wasn't too bold. It wasn't the kind of wink that puts you on the spot. Sometimes a wink can do that, it can make your brain freeze, you don't know what to do. But it was just a quick wink. Then he looked down to the counter, that's the important thing. Immediately after winking he looked down to the counter, right away. He didn't stay looking at me waiting for a reply wink or to see what I thought. He just gave me it. He gave me that wink with no expectation of anything in return, like a gift. Then he looked down.

And he called me 'mate'. He could have called me 'sir'. Some people like being called 'sir' or 'madam', it makes them feel like they're being treated with respect, like they're a member of the royal family coming to look at a factory or launch a ship. Some people like it because it creates a distance, which makes things a bit easier and less personal when complaints or demands are made, it makes it easier for both sides. But Stevie called me 'mate'. Not because he feels I'm undeserving of respect, but because he knows I don't need it. Nor did he do it to get familiar with me so that I feel uncomfortable making complaints or demands, but to make me feel like I can tell him anything. We're mates, after all. Not real mates, obviously, but for the duration of this wee thing we've got going on, we're mates just like any others.

Stevie's all right.

He beeps the barcode with his laser gun and reaches under the counter to pull out a poly bag. He flaps the bag up and down to open it up, but in doing so he wafts a leaflet off the counter and down onto his side of the floor. I watch him as he bends over to pick it up, and what I see makes me like Stevie even more.

It's not that I like him even more because I'm watching his arse. I am watching his arse, but that's not it, it's the whole thing. It's the way he's bending over. He's bending over in that bow-legged way, his knees slightly bent and pointed outwards, and his upper body bent right over. I don't know what it is about him bending over like that, it's like there's something open about it. I know that 'open' isn't the best word to use, because it makes you visualise him bent over with an open arsehole, but that's the only word that springs to mind. Open.

It's the way you imagine people to bend over in the wild, or in the jungle. You sometimes see programmes with Amazonian tribes where the men wear nothing but a wee piece of cloth tied around their waist. And every now and then, there's a shot of one of them from behind, somewhere in the background, bending over to pick something up. Cock, balls, arse, the lot, there it is, they don't give a fuck. They don't give a fuck because they've got nothing to hide. And that's the same with Stevie here.

I've sometimes seen guys like that in changing rooms, back in school, and in gyms when I got older. They're not stressing out trying to cover up their genitals with a towel, they know the sky won't fall if somebody catches a glimpse. With them, it's a towel between the legs, drying their no-man's-land with a heave-ho, heave-ho, right in front of you, mid-conversation. And I know they wouldn't mind if I did it as well. And why not? No formalities, no pretension, no lies, no borders, no barriers. Open.

Stevie's all right.

He picks up the leaflet, puts it back and goes to stick my thing in the bag. But then has a look at it.

'What is this anyway?' he asks.

'It's like a media streamer thing,' I say. 'You can put all your music and films on it and watch it from anywhere in the house. Hopefully.'

'Ah, right. I could do with something like that. I didn't know we had it. I suppose I should, since I work here!'

He has a wee laugh.

I love this guy.

It's the way he just laughed at himself for not knowing what his shop sells, even though he should. It's like he doesn't care. Not in a bad way, not in a cocky or arrogant way, but in a way that helps me relax and makes me less uptight about how the world should be.

Because there comes a point, I think, when you realise that the world isn't as orderly and in control as you might like it to be, that it's in fact held together with Blu-tack and Sellotape and the wheels are about to come off at any moment. It can be quite a scary realisation, that, enough to make most people panic. But here's Stevie here, and he's laughing.

We need people like Stevie. We need him to laugh, so that we can laugh. If you're ever stuck in a lift, or holed up in a loft to escape the zombie hordes, or looking through a telescope at the asteroid coming to wipe us out, you're going to need somebody like Stevie. You're going to need him to laugh. Because if Stevie can laugh, I can laugh. If Stevie doesn't care, I don't care. If Stevie can admit to a customer that he doesn't know what his shop sells, despite knowing that it could lose him his job, his wages, his house, his girlfriend, well . . . fuck it. Fuck it. In the happiest way possible, I say fuck it all.

Now Stevie's asking me if I want to buy something, something that I don't think I need, but I said yes. I don't know what it was; I wasn't really listening, I was smiling. Could have been batteries, even though the thing doesn't take them. Could have been some insurance thing that sticks an extra hundred quid on the price, even though I've already got insurance. Could have been anything. Fuck knows.

And fuck cares.

Cos see Stevie?

Stevie's all right.

THE FAKE

I have these burglars. They burgle my house.

Or so they think!

It started a while back. I can't remember the first time they did it, but they obviously enjoyed it so much that they decided to do it again, and again, and again. It must be like a pair of comfy old slippers. Each time they smash one of the windows and invite themselves in, well, it must be like a trip down memory lane for them. I can imagine them casting their minds back to that very first time, and all the times thereafter, reminiscing, telling stories, filling the house with laughter at my expense. Aye, I can just imagine them thinking about all those memories wrapped up in that very house.

And they'd be wrong!

See, I got myself an alarm. That's how it began. I decided to get myself an alarm, just to give these chaps a subtle indication that I didn't want them around, that I'd rather have the house to myself, thank you very much.

But when I went to the shop and saw the prices of these things, these alarms? Jeezo! The guy said to me, 'Well, you can't put a price on peace of mind.' But at that price? I think I'd rather be robbed! Then I said, 'Here, hold on, what are those alarms over there? They're not even half the price.' The guy told me that's because they were fake. Oh, I liked that. These burglars thinking my alarm was real when it wasn't, I liked the idea of that very much. The guy recommended against it, he recommended getting the real deal, but no no no. A fake one, please. That would show them. I don't like lying, but for breaking into my house, my private property, that's what they get.

Anyway, it didn't work. They must have seen right through it, the way those experts on *Antiques Roadshow* can spot a phony from a hundred yards. That's prisons for you: universities of crime, aren't they?

So I went back to the shop and complained. The guy said, well, he did recommend getting the real deal, and that it would have saved me money in the long run – a right smart arse. He tried to punt it to me again, the alarm, the real one, but this time he also advised me to get some cameras, all that CCTV carry-on. My God, if I thought the price of the alarm was bad, the cameras? He was obviously trying to get me while I was down, it was worse than being mugged at knifepoint. Then I said, 'Here, wait a minute, what are those cameras over there? Why are they so cheap?' And he told me it was because those were fake, just like the fake alarm. Oh, I liked that. He advised against it, but then again, he would: commission. No, I'll just have the fake one, if you please. I couldn't wait to get it home. I just imagined the burglars seeing the flashing red light and running for the hills. I just pictured them watching *Crimewatch* that night, biting their nails down to the knuckles, waiting for their faces to appear. But their faces wouldn't appear, because it was a trick! And it would serve them bloody right.

Anyway, it didn't work. I don't have a clue how they saw past that one. They must have gadgets to work it all out. Or maybe they've got somebody on the inside, in these shops, telling them how it all works in exchange for a share of the loot. However they did it, it was putting these burglars one step ahead, that was for sure. Always one step ahead.

But not any more!

No, I didn't buy a real alarm or a real camera, I told you how much that cost. But neither did I buy fake ones. I didn't buy a thing from that shop; no way I was going back there. So I built it myself.

I built a fake house!

I tore down the old one and built a new one right on top. You'd never know the difference. From the paint-work to the plumbing, the same in every way, inside and out. Except I don't live there.

I live in a tent!

And I watch them. I watch them burgle my house. Or so they think.

They take my telly, they take my computer, they lift out the furniture, my piano; anything that isn't nailed down, they take. And all that's real, that stuff is real, it's important that they don't suspect a thing. And so far, they haven't. Three times they've burgled my house, except they've not. Because it isn't my house.

I live in a tent.

It's cost me just over quarter of a million so far, I think. Maybe double, I'm not sure. But who's counting? Not me.

Because it's like the guy said.

You can't put a price on peace of mind!

VEGETARIANS

This was a nice wee restaurant, thought Doug. A nice place, with nice people. The staff seemed nice and so did the customers; they looked gentle. He looked at the menu, and a few words jumped out at him that explained the niceness, words like 'tofu', 'soya milk' and 'bean burger'. That's right, the place was vegetarian. 'Ah fuck,' whispered Doug to himself. He wasn't a vegetarian himself, and he fancied something with a bit of substance, something with a bit of meat, like pasta with some chicken, or maybe a steak pie. He knew it wasn't right to think like that. At least, it didn't feel right in here.

He always felt a bit guilty in places like this, and no wonder. He paid people to put animals in machines that tore them to pieces, and these good folk in the restaurant didn't. He could almost feel the guilt ooze out his pores like B.O. He looked around at them all, wondering if anybody had noticed his disappointment at the menu or heard him saying 'Ah fuck', but nobody had. He knew really that none of them would care anyway, he knew nobody really objected to being in the company of a meat eater – except for Morrissey or whoever – but he wouldn't blame them if they did. After all, how was it acceptable for him to cut a slice of flesh off an animal's arse and shove it in his mouth? How could he do such a thing? He loved animals, yet he had them killed, that was a bit Jekyll and Hyde, was it not? It didn't make sense, and it was probably the conclusion these folk around him came to a long time ago, when they decided to become vegetarians. It was such a logical, enlightened and kind-hearted decision. The decision to never kill again. The decision to love all living things, and therefore not to kill any living thing.

Except for lettuce, of course, haha.

That was funny. It was funny in that it was interesting. Doug paused for thought. He looked at the guy eating salad at the table nearby, a salad containing lettuce and tomatoes and other vegetables that used to be alive but now weren't. That was funny, now that he thought about it, because it's not as if vegetarians don't kill anything. They do kill, they just don't kill animals. But they kill plants. And that's all right, somehow. It's because plants are alive, but they're not alive like animals. Animals can think, they can feel, and that's what makes it wrong to kill them. Wrong in the eyes of vegetarians, that is. That's why the animals get to live and the plants have to die.

Doug wondered if things would be different if vegetables could think and feel. Like, imagine if scientists worked out that tomatoes could count to ten. Or imagine if when a potato gets peeled, it hurts like fuck. It was a gruesome thought, but it made Doug smile. However, his smile drifted off when he wondered if vegetarians applied the same thinking to people. Specifically, if vegetarians are all right with killing something that doesn't think and feel, what about if that thing that doesn't think or feel is a person? You get people like that. And Doug couldn't think of why those unthinking and unfeeling people would be exempt from judgement. After all, is vegetarianism not based in some way on the belief that human life is no more important than any other kind of life? If so, then why should human life be exempt from death, the same kind of death that befell every tomato, cucumber and carrot being scoffed by that guy at the next table?

Doug's smile had turned into a full-blown scowl.

He turned his head slowly and looked at the guy once more. Looked him up and down. Looked at his *ThunderCats* T-shirt, his crossed legs, his book. Such a harmless little man. Perfectly harmless. Unless, of course, you fell beneath the required level of intelligence one must demonstrate in order to not be put to death. And who decides upon that level? The vegetarians, of course. It could be a minimum IQ they have in mind. It could be the size or shape of your head. It could maybe depend upon the book you're reading (there's a thought). Or maybe you were walking down the street as a slate fell off a wonky roof above and right into your skull, putting you in an apparently unthinking, unfeeling state of being. Maybe you were born like that. Maybe to the outside world you are a motionless mute, but on the inside you have a vibrant, imaginative world, where you live in your own unique way. Well, I've got bad news for you: here come the vegetarians, and I'm afraid you don't matter a fuck.

Doug stood up, nudging his seat back behind him until it tipped over and onto the floor. He didn't bother picking it up, he just headed for the door. He couldn't bear another minute breathing the same air as these people.

And as he walked out, he remembered a wee fact he once heard.

Hitler was a vegetarian.

As he glanced back at them all, as he saw them all sitting at their tables – their desks – deciding which lives should live and which should end, that fact didn't surprise him.

No. It didn't surprise him at all.

NOTHING HAPPENS

Johnny and Paula were lying on the couch, watching the telly. *Coronation Street.* Johnny wasn't into it. He usually was, but something tuned him out, something had crossed his mind. He looked at himself, then Paula. He looked at the pair of them lying on the couch doing nothing. Then he looked at their empty dinner plates on the table. Then he looked at the wallpaper. Then he looked back to the telly.

'I've just noticed something,' said Johnny.

'What?' asked Paula.

'Something about this,' he said, pointing at the screen.

'Something about what? *Coronation Street*?'

'No,' said Johnny. 'Well, aye, but not just *Coronation Street*. All these things. Soap operas. Well, not just soap operas, programmes in general. Programmes with stories, I mean, not things like the news and the weather and that, I mean stuff like *Coronation Street*.'

'What the fuck are you talking about?' asked Paula,

not really interested in finding out. But he told her anyway.

He noticed that in all these programmes, soap operas, dramas, films, anything with a story, something always happens. You never get nothing happening. You never get an episode where nothing happens. Even when nothing appears to be happening, it isn't really. It isn't really nothing. There's always something to it, it's always interesting in some sort of way, or it's to tell you something about somebody, or it leads to something that'll happen later.

'Well, of course something happens,' said Paula. 'Something has to happen or nobody would watch it. Who'd want to watch something where nothing happens?' But that wasn't his point.

His point was that it was unrealistic. These programmes try to be realistic, things like *Coronation Street* or *EastEnders*, they try to be real, but they're not. He wasn't saying they were utterly unrealistic, they didn't have aliens or laser cannons or anything like that, but they just weren't like real life. Not really. In real life, not a lot happens. Or, at least, when interesting things do happen, they don't happen every single day. You get the odd interesting day, then you don't, sometimes for a good while. Sometimes fuck all happens for days on end. There had been times in his life when fuck all happened for weeks.

'What's your point?' said Paula.

He just thought it would be funny, and more realistic, if they had an episode of *Coronation Street* or *EastEnders* where fuck all happened. Fuck all interesting. Just nothing notable at all. Like, imagine if they had a few minutes of somebody putting their clothes in the washing machine. They don't accidentally put a red sock in with the whites or wash something that's dry clean only, they just put their clothes in the washing machine for however long that takes. Then imagine it cut to another character in a shop, thinking of what to get for dinner, picking tins of stuff off the shelves, having a wee look at the label, then putting them back. And it's not like you get to see what they're reading on the labels, it's not like they're reading the nutritional information and you see that the thing is high in sugar then that thing is given to a diabetic then there's a mad rush to the hospital. In fact, maybe you just see them go into a shop, but you don't get to go inside and watch, the camera just waits outside, like a dog, until the person comes out ten minutes later. Or maybe—

'Johnny, see seriously, gonnae fucking shut up?' said Paula, shaking her head. The shite he talked.

Johnny laughed, then shut up.

For a minute.

'Like, imagine something like this,' he said, looking at the two of them on the couch.

'Fuck's sake,' said Paula. 'Like what?'

'Like this,' he said. 'Like us.'

Johnny pointed out that this was real life, this right here, what they were doing right now. Johnny and Paula, right there on the couch, doing nothing, watching the telly, not saying a word to each other for almost half an hour, then having a wee argument. This was real life, this was realistic. Johnny thought somebody should write something like this, and stick it in on the telly, or in a film. Or in a book.

'Who'd want to read this?' laughed Paula, flicking through the channels to see what else was on.

'I would,' said Johnny. 'A story about nothing. I really like the sound of that.'

Paula said it sounded shite. Johnny said it didn't. He'd love to read something like that, a wee story about nothing. Somebody should do that, he said. Paula said nobody would do that because nobody would buy it. Something would have to happen otherwise they wouldn't even print the thing, they wouldn't make it. Try asking a bookshop to put your book on the shelves after telling them nothing happens in it, nothing interesting, like, seriously, nothing at all.

Johnny hoped that somebody would do it, somebody would write it. They'd probably get told by the publisher to put some big ending at the end to make all the nothingness worthwhile, but he hoped they'd stick to their guns and have the courage of their convictions and say, 'No, this is what happens. This is reality. This is real life.'

Paula had had quite enough of his pish for one night. She stood up, told him to remember to switch off the lights, then off she went to her bed. Johnny switched off the telly, but lay on the couch for a bit, still thinking about that book, that story. He wondered if anybody would ever write something like that, maybe about a guy just lying on the couch after his girlfriend has gone to bed. Lying there, doing nothing, not even watching the telly. Just lying there. Doing nothing. Nothing at all.

He waited until he heard Paula leave the toilet, then he stood up, switched off all the lights, then headed into the toilet himself. He picked up the tube of toothpaste and squeezed some toothpaste onto the toothbrush, then began brushing his teeth. That's the sort of thing he was talking about. Would anybody write something like that? Would anybody write about him brushing his teeth? Would they even go into detail about how he firstly picked up the tube of toothpaste and then squeezed some toothpaste onto the toothbrush?

He spat out the toothpaste, then looked at himself in the mirror. Could you write about this? Could you write about somebody just looking at themselves in the mirror? What about if it wasn't just a glance in the mirror, what if he was to look at himself in the mirror for ten minutes? Could he even look at himself for ten minutes anyway? He got out his phone, started the timer and gave it a go. He watched himself for one minute. After that, he waited another minute until it was two. Then it was three. Three full minutes of watching himself in the mirror. Not long after that, he realised he'd been looking at himself for four minutes, and before he knew it, it was five, the halfway point. Then, naturally, five became six, six became seven, and seven turned into eight. There was only two minutes to go until he had watched himself for the full ten. The next time he checked, that was it, it was ten minutes, he didn't even notice the nine-minute mark, the time had flew in.

He wondered if he should go for twenty minutes, then decided not to.

He went to bed and lay there, doing nothing. He did nothing other than think about how he'd just looked at himself for ten minutes, doing nothing, and how he was currently in bed, doing nothing. Absolutely nothing.

He yawned.

Then he yawned again. A doubler.

As he began to drift off to sleep, he wondered if a writer would one day come along and have the guts to write a story about nothing. A story that started with nothing, had nothing all the way through it, and ended with—

Just then, a laser beam the width of the sun blasted through planet Earth and destroyed everything before Johnny had time to complete his thought.

Some aliens at the other side of the galaxy were testing out their new weapon: the Doom Ray.

It worked!

DIRTY WEE SECRET

He was having a wank. That's what he was doing, that's why he locked the door, that's what he was up to in there. She wasn't daft.

He denied it, of course, he always did. She'd go to bed and he'd head to his wee home office, saying that he had one or two things to work on. And she believed him. Believed him until that time she caught him. She got up for a glass of water one night, and thought that while she was at it she'd pop her head in and ask him if he fancied a cup of coffee. You know, to help him get through his late shift, the poor wee soul that he was.

But the second her foot hit that squeaky floorboard outside the office door, she knew she'd been taken for a mug. The sound of him scrambling about, rattling the keyboard. Then her opening the door and seeing him in front of a switched-off monitor, his face beetroot. He said he'd finished for the night, and his face was red because he'd been doing press-ups. She was having none of it, and asked him why the fuck he was up wanking when he had a woman in the next room lying in bed. But he'd just deny it. Deny, deny, deny. She was taken for a fucking mug.

And after that, he put a lock on the door. He said it was because he sometimes wore headphones when working and if she walked in on him at night when he had them on then he'd get the fright of his life. Bullshit, he was having a wank. But again, he'd just deny it, deny, deny, deny. Denied it so much that she sometimes wondered, well, maybe he was telling the truth. But he wasn't. Was he fuck.

And tonight, she'd prove it.

He said he needed to get on with some extra work, surprise surprise, but she didn't cause a fuss. She just headed to bed, where she'd normally just fanny about on her phone for a while before nodding off. But not tonight. Because tonight she just happened to have left her phone next door in the office. How silly of her. She just happened to have left it sitting in the corner of the room, with the camera pointed at his computer, while running an app that enabled her to stream the live video to her tablet in the bedroom. Oopsadaisy.

She opened the bedside drawer and pulled out the tablet. She switched it on, tapped on the app and waited for it to load. She felt a bit grubby. She reminded herself of her mum, that time her mum read her diary when she was fourteen, and the argument that followed of who committed the greater crime: a fourteen-year-old smoking hash, or her mum for being a nosey fucking cow.

She decided to switch it off, to switch it off and give her boyfriend some privacy and respect, because this was out of order. She was just about to hit the power button when in kicked the video stream. And when she saw that, when she saw that grainy live feed of her boyfriend sitting down at his computer, well, all that human rights shite went right out the window.

It was like watching *Big Brother*. It was interesting watching somebody do nothing. And that's what he was doing: nothing. He really did seem like he was just working away, typing up some document. But after half an hour of that, things started to get a bit boring. There was the odd exciting moment when he'd open up a browser window, making her sit up in expectation of a wanking session. But no, just Wikipedia or some news article, all work-related. He didn't even waste some time on Twitter, she couldn't even nail him on that.

It was when she felt herself nodding off that she thought she'd better call it a night. Fuck waking up with him nudging her shoulder, pointing to the tablet by her side, still streaming the video from next door. Fuck trying to justify that. So once again, she put her finger on the power button of the tablet to switch it off. But once again, she had reason not to.

Her boyfriend had stood up and walked over to the office door to double-check the lock. This was interesting. He sat back down, looked over his shoulder, got up and checked the lock one more time.

This was it.

He sat back down, put on his headphones and undid his belt. So that's why you got the lock, you fucking liar. Not because you don't like to be disturbed while listening to music. You don't like to be disturbed while listening to shagging.

He looked over his shoulder one more time at the lock on the door, then faced his monitor. Then he pulled down his trousers and pants. It was going to happen. It was about to happen, and she wasn't sure if she wanted to see this after all. This was evidence enough. She should just switch off now. That was it, she really was going to switch off now. But once again, something stopped her. Something intriguing.

There was a mic on his headphones. She'd never seen him use it, but here he was, giving it a few adjustments so that it hovered just in front of his mouth – and that baffled her. If he was only going to watch a porno, what the fuck did he need a mic for? What sort of kinky shite had he got himself into?

She had to watch now. It was almost no longer about spying on her boyfriend, but a general case of human interest. Like when you watch a programme about men who like getting their balls trodden on by women in high heels. You have to watch, you just have to.

A video began playing on his monitor, but it didn't look like a porno. It looked like a game show, sort of. There was a presenter, and behind him scrolled hundreds of tiny screens, maybe thousands, each displaying a video of a man. Some of them were old, some young, some fat, some thin, all of them looking into the camera and all of them with their cocks out.

Honestly, what the fuck was this?

The presenter pointed at some screens behind him, half a dozen or so, making them whoosh to the foreground, all big. The presenter said something, and the men waved, happy to have been called out. She thought she recognised one of them, a guy she used to work with, but then they whooshed away.

Then another half a dozen were selected. One of them looked like Phillip Schofield. The absolute double of him. But it couldn't be, obviously, because this guy had his dick out and Phillip Schofield wouldn't do that. And then they too waved and whooshed away.

Just as she was about to take a moment to try and work out what she was seeing here, she saw something that made her heart skip a beat. Another half a dozen men flew out from the background to fill up the screen, and in amongst the range of men was her own. Her boyfriend.

'What the fuck?' she whispered.

Her boyfriend began to wave, the actual one in the home office, followed by the one on the screen. He was on a fucking webcam.

'Hello, everybody,' he said. Then he whooshed off.

'What the fuck?' she whispered again.

She watched the presenter continue to highlight group after group of men for another minute or so, until he seemed to bring that section to an end, and that it was now time to move on to what we all came here for. The camera cut to a close-up of the presenter as he said something serious, before turning to another camera and smiling again. When the camera cut back to the full-length shot of the presenter, she winced. The zip on the presenter's blue suit trousers was down, with his baldy cock and balls jutting out, his cock pointing high to the sky like a missile. It was huge.

The presenter held on to his cock and said a few words, prompting her boyfriend and all the other men on the screens to hold their cocks in unison. The presenter then raised his other hand in the air, paused for a moment, and then pointed at the camera. He shouted something, she couldn't hear, but she didn't need to. It was obvious from his mouth that he shouted 'Go!'

And they did. They went for it. Her boyfriend, the presenter and all these men. Shuffling.

Every now and then, a selection of men would whoosh into the foreground again, apparently at random, giving her a closer look at the participants of this online group wank. Some looked angry, like they'd been looking forward to this all week. Some looked chilled out like they were having a wank on a yacht.

A few of them started poking their arse. Then her boyfriend stood up and, without missing a beat, started poking his arse as well. The cable on his headphones wasn't long enough to enable him to stand all the way up, so he had to hunch over like a cyclist doing the Tour de France. A cyclist poking his arse. It put her mind in a spin.

Then she saw Chuck Norris. Or maybe it was Steven Seagal, she wasn't sure, but it was the guy from one of her boyfriend's action films. A famous guy. And it wasn't a guy that just looked like him. It was him. Poking his arse.

She saw an old guy she recognised from the park, jiggling his ballsack with one hand, and poking his arse with the other. She saw what looked like an Eskimo with his feet up in stirrups, poking his arse. She saw men from all over the world, and in various ways they were poking their arse.

When she saw the cream begin to seep out, she switched off. Cream she had never seen or heard of before, seeping out their arses. She looked to her boyfriend and hoped he wasn't the same. He picked up the pace, and before long, there it was. Cream, seeping out his arse, some of it down the back of his thighs, some of it dripping onto the floor. She imagined that it probably smelled pretty bad.

She switched off. She switched off the tablet.

She lay in bed, pretending to be asleep, until he came through to the bedroom an hour later. He put his arm around her, the same arm that was attached to the same hand that was poking his arse silly not long ago. She froze.

On the bus to work the next day, she saw men from the night before. Reading papers. Looking at phones. Being normal, like they don't poke their arse till it creams.

And during a meeting, she was introduced to a poten- tial client who had come up from London. She couldn't shake his hand. She hadn't seen him doing that thing, but she knew he had. She got a bollocking and was asked to give an explanation. She said she just didn't feel very well.

And she didn't. She knew what they did, what they all did, every last one of them. An ancient ritual? A new craze? She didn't know, but she knew they decided to keep it hidden in case it put the women off. And they were right. It was fucking horrible.

She knew she could never go back. Never go back home, never go back to before all this. It was too late. It changed everything and it ruined her life.

And that concludes the story.

And it is just a story. But I wonder. I wonder what message we could learn from her choices. Especially if you're a woman with a man in your life.

Like my girlfriend, for example.

Maybe the message is something like this:

If you do get up one night and hear me in the living room watching something on the telly with the sound down low with the light off and you're thinking of walking in, or maybe if I'm in our home office after saying I'm working late but you can't hear me typing anything so you're thinking of walking in, or maybe if I'm in the toilet for a really long time and you're thinking of putting me on the spot and asking me why I'm in there for so long, well . . .

Maybe it's best to just leave it.

AN IDEA

I've got an idea. This idea for something. A really good idea, in my opinion. It's the sort of idea I want to tell everybody about, but it's also the sort I want to keep close to my chest. The sort of idea that can be knocked. Stolen, by some scumbag. And then they'd get the credit, they'd get the pat on the back and everything else that comes with it. I don't think they'd get any money from it or anything, it's not like an invention, but, you know, if you were to come up with an idea for something, however big or small, and some scumbag comes along and swipes it and gets all the credit, that sort of thing can gnaw away at you for the rest of your life. So you can understand my reluctance. But I reckoned, well, if I put the idea in this book, if I just type it up and stick it in the book, it'll serve as a written record of who came up with the idea first and when. If somebody comes along later and says it was their idea, I can just pull out this book, show them the year it was written and that'll be them clamped.

But don't get me wrong, I'm not on some kind of ego trip here. I'm not expecting everybody to fall at my feet and call me a brainbox, I'm not expecting a statue. It would be a nice wee perk if that happened, I'm not going to lie, but that's not it, that's not what it's about. I just want people to know the idea was mine. Christ, that does sound like an ego trip, but honestly, it's not like that. It's complicated. I don't even think it's about who gets the pat on the back, now that I think about it. It's something else. It's hard to explain where the feeling comes from. Basically, the reason why it's so important to me that everybody knows it was my idea, and I know this is going to sound ridiculous, but it's because I'm Scottish.

You see, I grew up thinking that we Scots invented the world and everything in it. I was taught that that was our thing. Aside from kilts and bagpipes, that was our thing: inventing stuff. Every now and then, somebody would say, 'D'you know we invented that?' and you'd say, 'Really?' then you'd get this strange feeling of pride and accomplishment. It was strange because you yourself didn't invent it, but still, the feeling was there, because 'we' invented it. You'd be told that there would be no telly without John Logie Baird, and there you'd get that warm wee tickle in your heart. He was Scottish, you're Scottish, it's a Scottish invention, so, in a way, it's your invention – something like that. You'd be told that billions would have died without Alexander Fleming discovering penicillin. It'd make you feel like you had personally saved the lives of each and every one of them, that the world wanted to come up to you in the street and give you a big cuddle to thank you for the gift your people have given. You'd be told that they said the Forth Rail Bridge couldn't be built, yet it was. I don't really care about the Forth Rail Bridge, actually.

So many inventions, so many ideas and discoveries, so many reasons to have that feeling of pride or potential or whatever you'd call it. It's a good feeling, so I wasn't in any hurry to find out if it was justified or not, to find out if any of it was based on fact. I had no reason to doubt these things I'd been told for years by so many people. But it was only a matter of time before I started uncovering the truth.

John Logie Baird, for example. Turns out he didn't invent the telly after all, not really. He invented a sort-of telly. It was useless. It wasn't even an early version of something that was improved upon; it was a dead end, and some other guy came up with something much better. I won't bore you with the science, but in short, John Logie Baird's telly was shite. Then there's Alexander Fleming. I read up on him just a few weeks ago because, to be honest, I don't really know what penicillin is, I just knew that he was the first to discover it. But it turns out that's bollocks as well. Records show that other people discovered it decades before, it's just that Alexander Fleming was the first to, I don't know, get people interested in it or something. And as for the Forth Rail Bridge, we Scots show it off like it's some feat of Scottish ingenuity, but it was actually some English guy that designed it, I think, I don't know, I stopped reading. I don't really care about the Forth Rail Bridge that much.

The bottom line is that my Scottish pride lies in ruins. They built me up. They built me a castle. I never asked for a castle, but they built me one, they told me it was mine, that I could live in it, that I could point to it with pride and say, 'Look at me, this is what I've got.' And then my castle sank into the fucking quicksand. And now I feel like such a fucking mug.

And maybe that's why I want to share my idea with you today.

I want to restore a bit of that Scottish pride that's been taken, not in some kind of nationalist or *Braveheart*-y way, I don't want my fellow Scots to think that they're better than everybody else, nothing like that. I just want this to stop. I don't want some wee boy or lassie in the future, a Scottish boy or lassie, to have their confidence built on a lie, just for some bastard to tell them the truth, for some bastard to tell them, 'You'll never amount to anything, because nothing good has ever come out of Scotland, it was all a pack of lies.' I want them to be able to grab that person by the scruff of the neck, shove their face in my book and say, 'Look. Look right here. That other stuff, the telly, penicillin, you're right, it was all lies. But this idea, maybe the most important idea of the last century, this was his idea. His name was Limmy. And guess what? He was Scottish. I'm Scottish. So I can do anything.'

That's my dream. But of course, that won't happen unless I give you my idea. So, as much as I've still got my reservations about giving it away, here it is.

Here is my idea.

Imagine the day came that we here on planet Earth were to look through our telescopes and see, to our horror, that we were about to be invaded by a giant cat.

Don't send up missiles or fighter pilots in spaceships.

Use orange peels.

Know where all the satellites are? Just cover all that bit in orange peels.

Cats hate orange peels.

THE BILL

'Good afternoon,' said the call-centre guy on the other end of the phone. 'My name's Mark, how can I help you today?'

'Finally,' said Sean. It takes a fucking eternity to get through to somebody these days. It's the menus. Those fucking menus. Press one for this, press two for that. Sounds simple enough. All he wanted was to tell somebody that he was looking to pay his bill but he didn't have his account number handy. He pressed one to pay a bill, but what was the first thing it asked for? His account number. He just sat there doing nothing, waiting for the computer at the other end to realise the number wasn't coming, in the hope that it would pass him on to a human. But no, the computer just sat there at the other end, got itself comfy and waited it out. Eventually Sean just started pressing numbers on the phone, any old numbers just to move things on. The computer apologised and said that it didn't recognise that account number, and asked him to try again. No other option, no option to press another button to take him out of this, he had to rattle in another made-up account number, then again, until it finally washed its hands of him and put him through a living, breathing person.

'Finally,' said Sean again.

'Sorry, I hope you haven't been waiting too long,' said Mark. 'How can I help you today?'

'Hello, just phoning to pay my bill.'

'OK, can I have your account number please?'

'Well,' said Sean, 'that's the problem. I don't have it. Telling you, mate, see trying to get through those menus without your account number? Is this being recorded? Will they take a note of my feedback and get rid of those menus?'

'This isn't being recorded,' said Mark, 'but I understand, and I'll pass your feedback on. Do you know where to find your account number? It'll be on your latest bill, on the top right of the first page. Do you have that around?'

'Well, that's the other problem. Her. That's the main problem. I don't know where she's put it.'

Mark gave a polite laugh. 'I see. Well, if you ask her and then call back, we'll be able to get that bill paid for you, OK?'

'No, I don't want to go through those menus again, just gimme a minute and I'll have a look,' said Sean. 'Women, eh?'

Mark let out another polite laugh.

'Know what I mean?' laughed Sean.

Mark said nothing, and after a moment's silence, he could hear Sean open and close drawers and rustle about. A minute later, Sean returned. 'Nope,' he said.

'You can't find a bill?' asked Mark.

'Nope. Not one. No idea where she puts them, mate, no idea at all.'

'And she isn't in the house, I take it?'

'Nope,' said Sean. 'So I've got no idea. No idea where they are. I know where I put them, I remember where I put them, but then she goes and moves them to some other drawer, know what I mean?'

'Yeah, sounds familiar,' said Mark, and they had a chuckle. 'Hold on a moment, I might not need your account number, I'll just ask my supervisor.'

'Brain damage, aren't they?' asked Sean.

Mark said nothing.

'Brain damage, aren't they, mate?' asked Sean again, before realising Mark was probably away from the desk to talk to his supervisor. A minute later, Mark came back.

'Hi there, sorry about that,' said Mark.

'Brain damage, aren't they?' asked Sean, but Mark didn't catch it.

'What we can do is, do you have the phone you usually use to pay the bill? Your number's currently coming up as withheld.'

'I don't,' said Sean. 'My wife usually phones from her mobile, and I don't have her mobile, she does, so . . .'

Mark let out a wee tut.

'I know, mate,' said Sean. 'I know. Brain damage.'

'No, sorry, I didn't mean that,' laughed Mark. 'I was tutting at the situation, not your wife. I do apologise.' Mark laughed again. 'Thank God this isn't recorded. No, I do apologise.'

'It's cool, mate,' said Sean, laughing along. 'Seriously. It's her that caused the situation, know what I mean? I bet yours has caused a situation or two, eh? No offence, but you said it sounded familiar, did you not?'

'Yeah, a few situations. But I've caused a fair share myself.' Mark straightened up and got back to business. 'OK, let me think. How urgent is it that you pay the bill? Is it overdue?'

'What kind of situations?' asked Sean.

'Sorry?'

'Your wife,' said Sean. 'What kind of situations has she caused? Sorry to pry, but I could do with a laugh. I need it after today!'

'Oh, um, you know,' said Mark, half laughing. 'Just things like what you said, the same as yourself, moving things around, moving my keys, that kind of thing.'

'The keys! I know, mate, what's the script with that? It's like they get a buzz out of fucking with your head, isn't it?' asked Sean. 'Isn't it?'

'You could be right,' laughed Mark, before clearing his throat. 'OK, well, if your bill isn't that urgent, what you could do is—'

'Listen, mate,' said Sean. 'Listen.'

It was time to cut to the chase.

'You listening?' asked Sean.

'Yes,' said Mark.

'They're brain damage.'

'Yeah. But, if your bill isn't that urgent, you can wait until she—'

'Mate. It's cool,' said Sean quietly. 'I get it. I know what you're going through.'

'Sorry?' said Mark.

'Me and you. Me and you . . . are the same.'

There was a long silence from Mark's end. Sean continued, bringing his voice down to a whisper.

'They'd never make the connection. The police, I mean. They wouldn't have any records, my number's withheld. And this isn't being recorded, remember?'

Silence.

'There's nothing to connect yours to mine or mine to yours. They'd never think somebody would travel hundreds of miles just to do that. You're down south I take it, aye?'

Silence.

'Just think of the insurance. Has yours got insurance?' asked Sean. 'Life insurance? Get insurance. I know it's not about the money, but for all the shite we've had to go through we're entitled to some compensation, d'you not think?'

Silence.

'By the way, I'm not just some nutter.'

The line went dead.

Sean exhaled a big, long, fed-up breath, and looked down to his Yellow Pages. He drew a line through the company name and number and moved down to the next. He was almost at the bottom. It was taking fucking ages, this.

It's the menus, you see.

Those fucking menus.

THE JACKET

She stopped at the shop window for the third time that week. And how could she not? That jacket. Dark grey cashmere with a sumptuous silk lining, sparkling with an all-over sequin embellishment. It was divine. Oh, she hadn't worn anything like that in years, nor parted with that kind of money. £1,950, said the price. She shook her head. She could afford it, but then she wouldn't be able to afford much else. She had her priorities straight. Ha! Changed days.

She caught her reflection in the window. Yes, a lot had changed, both inside and out. There once was a day when all these things mattered, things like this jacket in the window, things like what she was pictured wearing, who she was pictured with and where. There once was a day when she cared more about those things than her own flesh and blood. When she gave up her son. Her baby.

But now her time in the spotlight was over, while her friends bathed in the love of their children and grandchildren. And here she stood alone at a shop window. On the outside looking in. She looked at her reflection once more and wondered if she had left it too late. Where was he now? Her boy. Did he have the same name, the one that she gave him? Did he have children of his own? Did they ask after their grandmother? Did he miss her?

She found out.

It wasn't easy. It wasn't as simple as typing his name into a computer and up came his address. Things were different back then. Back then, if you gave up your child, you gave them up, that was it. They were gone. It was what made them so easy to let go, and so hard to get back. So it cost her. Private investigators, the type of people she thought you'd only find in films. She hired one, who failed, then another, who also failed, until the third one managed to track him down.

Australia.

She wrote a letter, the old-fashioned way. He wrote back, and then they decided to meet. She bought a ticket, got on a plane, and off she went.

'It's me,' she said when he opened the door. 'It's Mum.' She spread her arms and welcomed his embrace. It must have been an unremarkable sight to any passers-by, a mum visiting her son, but it was the dream of saying those words that had kept her going when she felt like giving up.

She sat at his dining-room table as he handed her a cup of tea and a biscuit with a smile. They had some small talk. They chatted about the weather, the weather

Down Under, the weather back home. They chatted about her journey over and the films she watched during the flight. And he apologised for not being able to pick her up from the airport, due to work stuff getting in the way.

'Sorry,' he said.

Apologising for his career coming before his own flesh and blood.

'No,' she said, reaching across the table to hold his hand. 'I'm sorry.'

He laughed warm-heartedly and squeezed her hand back. He knew what she meant, but he told her it was fine. He knew that things were different in those days, there were fewer choices, there were expectations that women were required to meet. He understood, and it was fine, honestly.

But she apologised again. She apologised for depriving him of a mother, a mother to love and to receive love from. She regretted causing the pain he must have felt, the longing, but she hoped that today could be the start of making up for everything that was lost between them.

He wiped a tear from his eye. He assured her that he was never deprived of a mother's love. He had been blessed with a wonderful adoptive mum and dad who loved him as their own. He'd been very lucky.

She put her other hand over his, and gave it another squeeze, to tell him that she was here now. Mum's here.

He smiled, and said that everything had worked out in the end. In a way, it was better. Now he had two mums.

She pulled her hands away slowly.

He watched her hands leave, and asked if everything was all right. Did he say the wrong thing? She said she was just going to pick up her biscuit, that's all. He laughed.

She didn't.

Then he picked up his iPad and pulled his seat next to hers. 'So,' he said. 'How d'you fancy seeing your grandkids?'

She took a bite of her biscuit and nodded with a shrug.

He swiped through pictures of her grandchildren, pictures of them when they were babies, then when they grew into toddlers, then into teenagers.

She thought about how much it had cost for the plane tickets.

And the cost of the private investigators, including the ones that failed. And then there was the cost of the taxi from the airport because her son refused to pick her up.

Add them together and you're easily talking about £2,000.

About the same price as that jacket.

I HAVE SOME PICTURES

Hiya.

How are you enjoying the book so far? Thanks for getting it, I really appreciate it. In return, I'd like to do something for you. A favour.

You see, I have some pictures. Some rather compromising pictures that have come into my possession. Pictures of an adult, taken secretly and without consent, with the sole intention of causing the person embarrassment.

Pictures of you.

Now, I won't say what's in these pictures, I don't want to cause you any further discomfort, but I think you know what. Without spelling it out, it's that thing you sometimes do. OK, I'll leave it there, I think you know what I mean. I just want to move on to what comes next and how we can tackle this.

As I said, the pictures have come into my possession; I was not the person who took them. But I know the person who did. He is a disturbed and very damaged individual, but he's a professional. In short, this is what he does to pay the rent. All he wants out of this is cash. A lot.

Fortunately for you, me and this guy go back. We're by no means friends, but we do go back, and this person owes me. So I managed to cut you a deal.

He's asking for £100.

It's a fraction of what you would have to pay if I wasn't here, but I understand if it's still a bit steep. Which is why I'm going to pay most of it myself, to thank you for getting my book.

So all I need from you now is a tenner.

A tenner and this guy is gone.

Just hand it to me if you see me out and about, you'll recognise me from the picture on the cover sleeve. No need to stop and chat.

Anyway, enjoy the rest of the book, and I hope to see you soon.

All the best,

Limmy

WHY I DON'T COME HERE

Romy fancied some lunch, she was starving. She stood on the pavement, looking at the cafe across the road, before looking up the hill to her left. She wasn't sure where to go. The place she usually went to was a fifteen-minute walk up the hill, but she really couldn't be fucked with that, she wanted something now. But the cafe across the road, she didn't fancy that either. It was an all-right-looking place, but there was something about it she didn't like. It's not like she'd had a bad experience in there, she was pretty sure she'd never been in, but maybe that was it: it was unfamiliar. She stood for almost a minute, looking between the cafe and the hill, the hill and the cafe. Eventually she sighed and crossed the road to the cafe. She didn't want to, but she really was starving.

When she got in, she realised the place wasn't that unfamiliar at all. It was quite familiar, in fact. It had a homely feel to it, with its worn-down wooden tables and wine-bottle candlestick holders. She liked that look, but she didn't like it here for some reason, she just did not like this place. Had she been here before? Or did the decor remind her of somewhere else that she didn't like? She wasn't sure.

'Hi, what can I get you?' asked the guy behind the counter. Even he looked familiar, with his floppy hair and studenty way to him, but she couldn't say for certain if she'd seen him before or if, like the cafe itself, he just had a familiar look. A floppy-haired student. Ten a penny.

She turned around to look at the blackboard to see what was on offer, and noticed that she somehow knew instinctively where on the wall the blackboard was. Maybe she saw it on the way in. 'Can I have a cheese and ham toastie please?' she asked. 'And a tea?'

'No bother,' he said. 'Just take a seat and I'll bring it over.' So she sat down.

Her eyes wandered around the cafe, to the furniture, to the walls, to the counter, to the general shape of the place. And there was that funny feeling again. She had a feeling that she didn't want a cheese toastie after all. She had an urge to tell the guy to just leave it, that she'd changed her mind because she had to go and catch the train or something.

But why?

She tried to remember. What was it about this place? Did something happen? She couldn't remember the food being crap, or being shocked at the price, or the guy behind the counter being rude or moody. She wondered again if maybe she'd had a bad experience in another place that looked similar to here, but no, it was here. Whatever it was, it happened here.

Maybe, she thought, maybe the problem wasn't with the cafe, but with her. Did she do something the last time she was in that made her feel that she could never come back again? Did she come in here drunk one night and make an arse of herself? She started to feel ashamed, until she realised places like this shut about 6 p.m. No, she'd never been in here drunk, she'd never made an arse of herself in here at all. But she had been in here, she was sure of it, and something was telling her to leave.

She forced herself to forget it, to not even try to remember, her memory was shite. She looked around at the pictures on the wall to help her let it go. There were photos, paintings and drawings of Glasgow, just the usual stuff she'd seen in dozens of cafes about here, nothing out of the ordinary. Except . . .

One of them caught her eye.

It was an old black-and-white photo, of this very cafe, taken from across the road. She didn't know how old it was, but it was old enough for there to be a cobbled street outside. Every man on the street was wearing a hat. Every woman had a long, flowing skirt that came down to their feet. It was that old. Could it be . . .?

She heard the guy behind the counter approach her, but she didn't turn to look. She couldn't take her eyes off the photo. She thought she knew why. But that would be ridiculous, wouldn't it? She didn't believe in any of that.

She remembered seeing a hypnotist do it one night. A hypnotist came to her local and did a show, the standard routine of making people bark like dogs or making them believe their seats were on fire. But at the end of the night, he said he'd like to show another side of hypnosis: the ability for hypnosis to help delve deep into forgotten memories, not just from this life, but from past lives that have gone before. She watched as her mate sat on a seat in front of the pub, her eyes closed, talking conversationally about her life in Ancient Egypt. It was amazing to watch, but did she believe it? No. Of course not. Now, though, she wasn't so sure.

But how would that explain the familiarity of the guy behind the counter? Or the position of the blackboard on the wall?

She snapped out of her trance as the plate was put on the table.

'There you are,' smiled the guy, 'one cheese and ham toastie, and I'll just get your tea.'

She smiled back, and watched the guy return to the counter, dragging his feet behind with a scuff, scuff, scuff.

She picked up her toastie, but her attention returned to the photo on the wall once again. She felt herself being pulled in, only to be pulled out with the sound of that scuff, scuff, scuff of the guy from the counter coming over with her tea.

'And here's your tea,' he said. 'Enjoy.'

'Thanks,' she said.

And off he scuffed again. Scuff, scuff, scuff, scuff, scuff . . .

Scuff, scuff, scuff, scuff, scuff, scuff, scuff . . .

. . .

. . . scuff, scuff . . .

. . .

. . .

. . . scuff . . .

. . . scuff, scuff, scuff, scuff, scuff . . .

. . . scuff, scuff, scuff, scuff, scuff. Scuff, scuff. Scuff, scuff, scuff, scuff . . .

. . .

. . .

. . .

. . . scuff.

She remembered now.

THE BREAK-IN

I've got a mate, Roddy, who told me about a break-in he had a few weeks ago. It's only now he felt he could speak about it, and I can understand why, because what happened was pretty fucking bad.

He told me that he heard a sound coming from his kitchen in the middle of the night, but that was nothing new. He had this dishwasher with a special feature where it would pop the door open when it was finished, letting all the steam out. So if he heard a sound coming from somewhere in the house, he'd just assume it was that. But this night he thought he could hear something else. The floor creaking. And mumbling.

He picked up a fork that was sitting on his bedside table – it was the only kind of weapon he could find – and he headed out the room. He told me that, in hindsight, he should have just stayed in there and hid under the bed. But he went out into the hall. Nobody was there, and he couldn't hear anything coming from anywhere else in the flat, so he thought it was maybe nothing. But when he opened the living-room door, somebody shone a torch in his face then hit him with it over the head.

He remembered decking it, and being held down by somebody. Then a lamp got turned on, and he could see that there were two guys. Both of them had their faces covered with scarves and they had their hoods up. The one that was holding him down asked him where his bank cards were and got Roddy to tell him the PINs, before telling the other one to fuck off to get the money out the bank. The one that was holding him down found the fork and held it to Roddy's face, telling him that if he tried to move then he'd take out his eyes.

When the other guy was away to the cash machine, the guy that was holding him down pished on the floor. Roddy said he didn't know if the guy was trying to humiliate him or if he genuinely needed to pish without taking his eyes off Roddy, but either way it was degrading. It created a puddle on the laminate floor, and Roddy was face down in it. And he couldn't move away because of the fork at his eye.

When the other guy came back, the one holding him down stood up and booted Roddy in the chest. He told him that if he tried to report any of it to the police then the pair of them would come back and kill him; they knew where he lived.

Pretty fucking bad.

Anyway, I got myself one of those dishwashers, they're magic. I didn't know they existed until Roddy told me.

With my old one, you had to open the door manually, and if you forgot, all the steam turned back to water, leaving the dishes wet.

Now they're bone dry and can go straight into the cupboard.

BEHIND THE TOILET WALL

There once was this guy doing a shite. Let's call him Donnie.

He was doing a shite in the toilet in his house. Trying to, anyway, but he had a feeling he was in for a wait. It was going to be one of them. One of those right tearjerkers. He was fine at the moment, but he knew that somewhere down the line, in maybe five, ten, fifteen minutes, things were going to get hard. He didn't want to think about it, so he thought about something else. He looked at his fingernails, then looked at the floor. Then he looked straight ahead, then back to his nails. Then he looked to the tiles on the wall, the ones to the right, above the bath. And that's where his mind stayed. God, he hated those tiles.

The tiles were purple, ugly as fuck, but they were nothing to do with him. He'd only moved in about six months ago, and despite the effort he'd put into doing up the rest of the house, he never got round to doing up the toilet. It was low priority, as far as he was concerned, hardly the most important room in one's home – it's the room you shite in, after all. But it was a bit of an embarrassment when he got people round. He'd always have to get his excuses in quickly before they wandered off to the toilet, explaining that he hadn't got round to doing it up and that he knew it was a state, just in case they actually thought he was responsible for it or that he planned on keeping it like that because he was into it. They really were that bad, the tiles. What was worse was that they were only on that one wall. It would be bad enough if it was purple all around, but the fact that all the tiles in the toilet were white except for this one wall, it just somehow made it worse. Maybe it was because the purple stood out more against the white, but it was probably because the white tiles showed you how good it could have been, and then you got this big ugly wall of purple that ruined everything. Why the fuck did they do that? Maybe that was the worst thing, the mystery, wondering what possessed them to go and ruin a perfectly good—

One of the tiles moved.

That's what it looked like anyway. He didn't know which tile moved, if any, but it felt like one of them had changed their angle slightly, showing a slightly different reflection of the toilet than before. It could have just been him moving on the toilet, but he wasn't sure that he did move. It could have been his neighbour. Maybe his neighbour went into his toilet next door and the weight on the floor somehow had a knock-on effect on the wall, and . . . no. His neighbour wasn't on that side, his neighbour was behind the wall to the left of where he was sitting. Behind the wall to the right, the purple one, was, well, he wasn't quite sure.

He opened the toilet door while remaining seated on the pan, and leaned around slowly for a look, for a wee reminder, being careful to not nip the half-inch of shite poking out his arse. The toilet was halfway between the upstairs and downstairs. He could see the kitchen downstairs, and that its ceiling probably came to about halfway up the purple tiles. Then he looked upstairs and saw that his bedroom was probably behind the top half. Except . . .

He raised his finger to point at the level of the upstairs floor, where his bedroom was, then he drew an imaginary line from there to inside the toilet and along the purple wall.

Hold on. Hold on a second here. That's strange.

The bedroom floor seemed to start quite a bit higher than halfway up the toilet wall, like there was some kind of gap between the kitchen ceiling below and the bedroom floor above. Not just a wee gap for the pipes and electrics, but a gap of considerable height. About the height of a dog, and a Great Dane at that. That's hell of a strange. He wondered if he was just being stupid and filling his head up with interesting thoughts to divert attention from the task at hand. But there was no doubt about it, there was something behind those tiles. There was a gap unaccounted for. What the fuck is that, man? That's freaky. So freaky that the shite that was making good progress out his rear end just stopped. It just hung there, as if it was as freaked as he was.

Then he heard the tapping.

It was slow at first. Just one tap, then silence. Then another, and another, then silence again. He told himself that it was just the pipes or something. His neighbour had put the heating on, that's all, and pipes do that when they're heating up, they expand or whatever it is. It didn't explain why the tapping sounded like it was happening directly onto the tiles from behind, but it had to be something like that. It had to be. He was happy with that explanation, and he was looking forward to finishing his shite and getting out of there.

Then he heard the scratching.

It began with a tap, then it screeched like a fingernail being dragged down a blackboard. Then it stopped. Then it started, this time with another: two fingernails, or two something else. Maybe three. Donnie struggled to find an explanation, but he was still happy to accept that it was just something to do with the pipes, he'd settle for that. He'd like to just go now. He almost felt like apologising for his curiosity, but apologise to who? To what? He didn't know. He was kind of losing it here.

Then it stopped.

Silence. Donnie sat in silence. After a minute, he exhaled, not realising he'd been holding his breath.

He was absolutely shiting himself. Not literally, because that shite just would not budge until this thing was over. He didn't quite know what was going on, it really was freaking him out a bit, maybe it was because he was in a compromised position. Maybe the pressure of the shite against his veins had somehow fucked with his head, like heatstroke or the bends. He tried taking his mind off things. He looked down at his fingernails again, and wondered if maybe that's what the scratching sound was. That's probably what it was. The tapping was his foot, and the scratching sound was just—

Donnie heard creaking, then the sound of a tile falling into the bath to his right.

He could sense that something was moving, but he didn't look. He didn't fancy it, to be honest.

Then another tile fell, then another, then two or three at a time. Tapping, scratching, creaking and smashing, until eventually there was silence. Silence for who knows how long. Two minutes? Two hours? Silence.

Donnie shut his eyes, and turned his head towards the right, towards the purple tiles, or where they used to be. Towards the breathing. Then, for reasons unknown to me, he decided to open them.

In the hole in the wall was a cow with seven legs. Its head was boneless. On the left side of its face was a vagina, hanging from which was a tongue with teeth on the end that chewed at nothing. On the right was its only eye, held half shut by matted eyelashes and congealed pus. It had a cock the size of a two-litre bottle of cola, raw and rotten like a peeled plum, crawling with flies and larvae that made the cow moo in pain. Its udders hung below like a ballbag.

Donnie died from a heart attack, fell over and finally actually did shite himself. Literally.

And do you know who Donnie was?

Elvis.

This story was about Elvis.

THE WEREWOLF

Every full moon, he changed. He was a werewolf. You wouldn't notice him if he walked past you in the street, he looked like any other guy.

But the following morning, he would change back, back into his natural form. A wolf. A wolf in a Travelodge room.

No recollection of how he came to be wearing human clothes. Nor of the newspaper lying under his paw, the crossword complete. Or of the toast crumbs on his chest.

The toast crumbs.

Oh my God, the toast crumbs!

What did he do last night?

ARNOLD'S ARSE

Arnold went to the hospital. He had to. He walked up to the woman behind the counter and told her what was up, that he was having trouble passing solids. She asked him to elaborate, was he constipated? Arnold said it was worse than that, and he explained. She asked him to repeat that, she couldn't quite hear him. He looked over his shoulder to make sure nobody was listening, then leaned in closer and told her again. Aye, that's what she thought she heard the first time, but she'd asked him to repeat himself because what he said was preposterous. But now that he'd said it again, she concluded that he must be on something, and asked him to take a seat.

He sat in the waiting room until she called out his name and told him what room to go to. When he got there, a doctor asked him what seemed to be the problem. Arnold told the doc, and the doctor also concluded that Arnold must be on something, but he asked Arnold to pull down his trousers and pants anyway to have a look.

'My word,' said the doctor, looking at Arnold's behind. He could see immediately what the problem was. Arnold's arse was one big bum cheek. There was no hole. It was like a big thumb.

The doc asked him to wait there as he headed off to get another opinion. Arnold sat there wondering what was going to happen. He hoped it would be pretty easy to fix, maybe he could even get up the road that night in time to watch a film. The doctor came back with half a dozen colleagues, who took turns in having a look at Arnold's arse. Each of them shook their head and mumbled medical stuff to the rest. Arnold stood there quietly, out his depth, like a dog at the vet's.

'Excuse us,' said the doctor, and Arnold was left alone in the room once more, this time for half an hour. He started to realise that maybe this was more serious than he thought. The doctor returned and asked Arnold to come with him; they were going to take him for some scans. They headed out the room and down the corridor.

'So d'you think I'll need an operation or something?' asked Arnold.

'It's too early to say, but once we get the scans we'll have a clearer picture of what the issue is,' said the doctor, putting a hand on Arnold's shoulder.

'It's just that I was hoping to get up the road tonight in time to watch a fi—'

A bolt from a cattle gun straight to the head, and down he fell. Then off to the incinerators he went.

Well, what else could they do? They'd never seen anything like it. An arse without a hole? An arse that was one big bum cheek, like a big thumb?

Gives me the heebie-jeebies just thinking about it.

THE CONCERT

He was sitting at the concert, looking around, waiting for the thing to start. The place was a bit of a dive. Not the best place, but not the worst either. Just another featureless, multipurpose arena, built on the cheap, lined with hard, plastic seats bolted into concrete. He looked down and saw that his own seat had been vandalised by a lighter. He looked at the floor. It was dotted with circles of chewing gum, all blackened by footprints and dirt. And he knew that there was a crushed can of Sprite under his seat that the cleaners either hadn't spotted or couldn't be bothered picking up. No, it wasn't the worst of places, but it wasn't exactly deluxe. And it was a far cry from what this chap was used to.

The Royal Albert Hall, that's what he was used to, that's the kind of place where you were more likely to see him. Well, this time last year, anyway. There he'd be in one of those private boxes, with champagne on ice by his side, dressed in a suit that cost more than your motor, before leaving at the end of the night in a motor that cost more than your house. The high life, that's how he liked to spend his money, that's what drove him to earn it. He wanted the best in life, the finest in life. Food, wine, the company that he kept, the watch that he wore, the yacht. He was a man of extremes. The uppermost prestige and taste, that's what he was all about. All that.

Somebody behind him burped, then a woman laughed. He wondered if they were drunk, and it worried him, but he relaxed when he realised they probably weren't. It just wasn't the done thing at a concert like this. There were children here, families, couples, nice people, chatting away or singing songs or just sitting quietly, arm in arm. It was all very civilised, just the way he liked it. He turned around for a glance, and saw that the couple looked as sober as anybody, sucking up their big plastic cups of Diet Coke. That's all right then. He felt overly sensitive, but he just didn't think it would be good to have people like that around him. Drunks, or worse. Not that he was a prude. Far fucking from it.

See, there had come a point when he got tired of the high life. After all, a wine could only be so fine. A good suit could only be so good. A watch was a watch was a watch. He'd reached the top, there was no place higher, and for a man of extremes, there was only one place left to go: down. He was never one for drugs, so it began with gambling. Huge stakes on red or black, huge losses, huge wins. The thrill of it. And with the thrills came the thrillseekers, the hangers-on, the vultures circling the guy blowing all his cash. Then finally, fuck it, then came the drugs. Then came the drugs! The yacht parties. The pills, the coke, the crystal meth, morning, noon and night, all around the clock. He'd wake up with everything gone, everything taken, and do it all over again. He torched the yacht. His posh mates turned their backs on him, he was turned away from places he'd been going to for years by doormen he was on first-name terms with, there were fights and black eyes. He was an outcast, freefalling, on a collision course with rock bottom. He got in his motor one night and went looking for a wall to crash into or a bridge to fly off. He'd reached the highest highs and the lowest lows. Both extremes. What else could a man like him do?

The lights in the concert began to dim; the crowd cheered, and then settled. The band were about to come on. The band that saved his life.

As he headed his motor towards a lamppost, a song came on the radio. It took a moment to realise the significance of what he was hearing, but when he did, he swerved back into lane. It was 'End of the Road' by Boyz II Men. He pulled over, turned off the engine and listened to it from start to finish. It was a song he'd heard on the radio since the Nineties; he neither liked it nor disliked it, it was nothing to him, yet now it meant more to him than perhaps to anybody else listening at that time. But no, it wasn't because he was at the end of the road in terms of his life, or that he'd reached the end of the road in terms of his exploration of the extremes, or because he was going to literally end himself on a road. The song had given him a new purpose, a new extreme, and one that wouldn't leave him disillusioned or self-destroyed.

The Boyz took to the stage. His view wasn't brilliant, sitting near the back and to the side, but it was all right. They started with a few of their new numbers, attempts to bring themselves up to date with new production sounds, which, judging by the faces in the audience, not a lot of people went for. Eventually, they moved on to their old familiar tunes, the fans sang and clapped along, and he joined in as much as he could. As it got near the end, the energy of the crowd had subsided and some of them were looking at the time. And then finally, after the Boyz said goodnight and walked off, they walked back on to play the song that most people had been waiting for – he'd certainly been, as it was the song that had brought him here tonight: 'End of the Road'. However, their live version didn't sound nearly as good as it did on the radio. They dodged some of the trade-mark high notes, due to them being a wee bit over the hill, plus he heard somebody mention that they didn't sound the same now that one of the singers had left. He agreed. All in all, it just wasn't a very good night. It was adequate. It was average. Yet it was one of the most extreme experiences of his life.

It was extremely mediocre. Extremely bland. Extra-ordinarily ordinary. It was normal with a capital N, to the nth degree. It was everything he hoped it would be.

Right down to the chewing-gum floor and the vandalised seat. It was wonderful.

A whole new world had opened up to him, one that he could never become disillusioned with or self-destruct over. How can you become disillusioned with something you already know to be not that good? How can you self-destruct over Boyz II Men, or whatever else he planned to get into? Which made him wonder: what next? What extremely run-of-the-mill thing could he see or do next? Maybe he could get tickets for one of those Rat Pack tribute bands. Or maybe go on a coach tour. Or maybe watch a romcom, the kind you see advertised on the side of a bus.

He had such an adventure ahead. But what if he grew disillusioned with that? What if his mission to explore the extremes of mediocrity became mediocre in itself? What an exciting prospect!

He stood up and joined the queue to leave. A stranger asked him if he'd enjoyed the show. He said it was all right. He asked the stranger if he enjoyed the show. The stranger said it was all right.

The night had already been perfectly mundane, but that was the icing on the cake.

ARNOLD'S ARSE EYE

Arnold had a problem: he had three eyes. Two were in their usual place, but the third, well, that was somewhere else. No, it wasn't in between the other two. No, it wasn't on the back of his head, or sticking out the top on the end of a tentacle.

It was in his arse.

He didn't always have it, not that he was aware of anyway. He only found out about it when he went to the doctor for a check-up, the kind they ask men to go for after they reach a certain age, the one where the doctor puts on a glove and sticks a finger up and has a feel about.

'I can feel something,' said the doctor. 'Just let me have a closer look.'

Arnold didn't like the sound of that, it sounded pretty bad. But it was nothing that he or the doctor imagined. The doctor had a look inside with his torch, and got the fright of his fucking life. He staggered back and collapsed against a cabinet, then he gave Arnold the news.

'There's an eye up your arse, Arnold. An eye.'

Arnold couldn't believe it. Well, you wouldn't. He asked for a second opinion from another doctor in the surgery but it was the same again. She had a look, got the fright of her life, collapsed against the cabinet and told him there was an eye up there. Arnold didn't believe her either, and so it went on, with a third, fourth and fifth opinion, opinion after opinion until everybody in the building had had a good look. Arnold even got the patients in from the waiting room to have a gander, in case all these doctors were at it, but they too did the same. Arnold looked at them all, doctors and patients alike, as they lay there in a pile at the bottom of the cabinet, and he finally accepted the truth. He had to, for he realised he was looking at them with the eye in his arse.

He asked everybody to leave, so that he could chat with his doctor in private. 'So, what are my options?' he asked. The doc said he could have the eye out immediately, right there and then, the sooner the better; it was an abomination. Arnold was about to give the doc the nod when he wondered if he could maybe have a bit of fun with it first. The doctor reluctantly agreed to let Arnold go for a wee half-hour wander, but he must return before the clock struck three, or the eye would turn into a pumpkin. Arnold couldn't believe his ears. A pumpkin? The doctor told him he was only joking, but he'd really like him back by about three. Arnold left, excited about all the things he was going to do in this final thirty minutes with his arse eye.

The first thing he did was a shite, to watch the shite pass his eye and plop into the pan below. That was good.

Then he had sex, anal sex, and watched the cock go back and forth like something out of a 3D film. And that was good as well. But after that, he was out of ideas. Except one.

He had the idea to stand in front of an oncoming bus, then pull down his trousers and pants and show the driver his arse. The driver would think Arnold was about to get hit because he wasn't looking behind him, but Arnold would rely on the eye in his arse to gauge how close the bus was before jumping out the way. The driver would be amazed.

So with a few minutes left in his half-hour playtime, Arnold walked onto the road and flashed his arse to an oncoming bus. His vision was perfect, his arse eye was twenty-twenty. But the problem with just having one arse eye is that you can't judge distance very well. You need two eyes for that. So he left it too late. But it wouldn't have mattered anyway. When he tried to jump, he tripped because his trousers were round his ankles, and he got demolished.

I think the worst thing that ever happened to Arnold was finding that eye in his arse.

PUMP

Typical, thought Joe. The one day he goes out cycling without either a spare tube or a pump is the day he gets a puncture. It just had to fucking happen today, didn't it? And the funny thing is, he deliberately left the tube and pump in the house in the hope that it would help him cycle just that wee bit faster. The tube, the pump, the bottle of water, the Allen keys, all the essential bits and bobs that they tell you to never leave the house without, all left in the house, for the sake of lightening his load by no more than a fraction. It was stupid, it was risky, but he hadn't had a puncture for well over two years, and had no reason to think that today would be the day that the planets aligned to take the total piss out of him.

He wondered how long he'd have to walk. He remembered what the cycle route looked like on the map before he left the house. It was one big fuck-off canal path that went on for twenty miles, occasionally passing by a wee village, but mostly passing through nothing but fields.

He got out his phone and opened up the map, hoping that he was just five minutes away from a train station or something. But no. A forty-five-minute walk to the nearest town, and no sign of a train station either. He shook his head. No doubt it would start bucketing down into the bargain, the way his fucking luck was going. And to think he got himself into this because he wanted to go faster. Haha. He was going fucking nowhere.

'D'you want a pump?' came the voice behind him.

Joe turned around to see who was speaking, and had to stop himself from smiling. It was a woman. A good-looking woman, he thought. She looked fit and athletic. Her face was shiny with sweat, her cheeks were red, and the way she was heavy breathing made her look like she was blowing him a kiss. In short, she looked pure sexy. And she'd asked him if he wanted a pump.

'Cor,' said Joe, 'you don't waste any time, do you, sweetheart?'

No, he didn't really say that, don't worry. But the thought did pop into his head. It was an unpleasant surprise. He didn't know where it came from, he never considered himself to be a sleazeball. He wasn't, he was sure he wasn't, yet here he was, with a thought that wouldn't be out of place in a *Carry On* film. He wondered if maybe that's all it was, maybe he'd watched one too many *Carry On* films when he was younger, and it just seemed like the most natural punchline to that kind of setup. But that was a cop-out, because it wasn't a setup, this was real life, and he knew it.

He was fucking ashamed. He felt like a thirteen-year-old. He felt like some immature schoolboy that can't have a conversation with a female without spunking in his drawers. But he wasn't thirteen, he didn't have that excuse. He was a grown man who should know better. All that stuff about her looking fit and athletic and blowing him a kiss, Jesus fucking Christ. You've got a puncture, mate, and a helpful cyclist (who just happens to be a woman) stopped to see if you need assistance. She wants to know if you want a loan of her bike pump, that's all.

Or is it?

Is that all it is? Maybe, just maybe, she doesn't really mean a bike pump. Maybe she really does mean that other type of pump. A pump-pump.

Oh my God. I can't believe you're thinking that. Just tell her to go. Tell her to go right now, tell her you're dangerous and she should cycle away as fast as she can. Tell her you're a sleazeball and you can't understand why a woman would talk to you other than to initiate sexual intercourse.

No, he thought. Let's keep an open mind here. Aye, it's narrow-minded to think she must be after a shag, but it could be argued that it's also narrow-minded to assume that she isn't. Women have a sexual dimension just like you, mate, and for you to find it strange that a woman would wish to act upon that is . . . well, it's sexist. It's actually sexist. Maybe she's genuinely asking if you fancy a shag. Maybe she's using the bike pump thing as a double-meaning thing, to get the conversation

going, so that she can chat for a while first, work out
if you're what she's after, and then, if you're not, back
out of the whole thing by saying that she only meant
a bike pump. Think about it, why is she offering you
a pump when you've probably already got one? What's
the use in her offering a pump without also offering a
spare inner tube? If she thinks you've already got a
spare inner tube, what would you be doing with that
without also having a pump? The situation doesn't make
any sense unless you see it from the point of view of
her asking you if you fancy a shag. You thought the
planets were aligning, well, maybe they are, but not to
take the piss out of you. They're aligning to get you
your hole.

Or maybe, you utter fucking sleazeball, she's just asking
if you want a bike pump for your flat tyre. Now tell her
you're fine, thanks, and let her get the fuck out of here.

'I'm fine, thanks,' he said.

She smiled. 'All right,' and off she cycled down the
canal path ahead. He began walking in that direction
himself, keeping his eyes to the ground to avoid looking
at her arse; he'd sickened himself enough today already.
When he could no longer hear her tyres against the dirt,
he felt it was safe to look up.

And there, in the distance, he saw her stopping to say
something to a middle-aged guy in wellies walking his
dog. The guy looked over his shoulders, left and right,
then nodded at her. He tied the dog's leash to a branch;
she got off her bike and led him into the bushes.

When Joe eventually caught up with them a few minutes later, he had a wee peek. Looked like he was right about the planets aligning to take the piss out of him after all. The pair of them were going at it hammer and tongs.

Joe was gutted. It looked fucking brilliant.

CHEAT

There once was a man who was shite at playing games. The kind you play on your phone. Puzzle games, action games, you name it. His skillz were laughable.

So he decided to cheat.

He got some apps that made him shit hot; he felt fantastic, top of the world. But then he realised it was all just pretend. It was all in his mind. He wasn't actually good, he was just imagining he was. And if he was just imagining he was, why bother even playing the game in the first place? He may as well just imagine that as well.

So he did.

He put down his phone and simply imagined himself playing. It was a brilliant idea. It cut out the middleman. It cut out the middleman of staring at a screen for half the day, plus it saved him a few quid, because he could play any game he liked, games that didn't even exist, and it cost him nothing. He imagined himself winning over and over, and in a far shorter time than if he was winning in real life. In real life, even the shortest game would take at least a minute. In his mind, he could convince himself he was winning ten games a minute. Or a hundred games a second. It was up to him. It put a right spring in his step, it was so fucking easy.

Too easy.

He needed a challenge. He needed to imagine at least some sense of achievement, some sense of there being a battle against the odds. So he lost a few games. Not many, to begin with. Every thousand wins or so, he'd chuck in a loss, to balance it out. It hurt, but not enough. So he chucked in some more. A loss every few hundred. Then a loss every fifty. Then a loss every ten. Before long, he lost as many games as he won, it was fifty-fifty.

And soon after that, he was on a total losing streak. He was back to being shite.

His skillz were laughable.

So he decided to cheat.

THE BEAR COSTUME

These people that run marathons wearing a bear costume, it's incredible. Not only running twenty-six miles non-stop, but huffing and puffing inside a big furry suit. All that body heat having nowhere to go. Plus there's the weight itself holding you back, it must be a nightmare. And I should know.

I think it was about a month ago, I was in the motor at the traffic lights one afternoon, and crossing the road was somebody in a bear costume. They had the full thing, the suit, the head, the lot, like a big teddy bear. It wasn't a marathon or some other kind of race, I didn't know what the occasion was, and I'm quite sure nobody else knew either. But that didn't stop passers-by going in for a cuddle and a picture. It didn't stop my fellow drivers beeping their horns and waving in the hope of getting a wave back. When the light went green, I quickly rolled down the window to give the bear a wave myself, and when it waved back to me, I was delighted. I'm a grown man, but I have to admit it, it gave me a right wee buzz.

As I drove away, I looked in the rear mirror and saw what the occasion was. A lassie had appeared from a pub with a pink bucket, and began walking alongside the guy in the costume. They asked a few folk around to chuck in some coins, before heading into another pub nearby – they were collecting for charity, obviously. I thought that was really good of them, I felt good will towards them. Funny thing was, I felt good will towards that teddy anyway, even before I found out the person inside was doing it to raise money. And that, to me, was quite a revelation.

None of us knew. Back when people were going in for their cuddles and we were beeping our horns and waving, we didn't know it was anything to do with charity. We didn't know why that person was in a bear suit. It wasn't Pudsey Bear from Children in Need. It wasn't some famous bear we all knew and loved, like Paddington Bear or Bear in the Big Blue House or thingy from *Rainbow*. It was just a bear. Yet we all had love for it. We all sent our warm feelings and best wishes to this complete stranger. And I thought, Here, I could really do with that.

Things haven't been going too well recently. I've not exactly been having a lot of warm feelings or best wishes coming to me, not from strangers, not from friends either. I've fallen out with one or two of them, plus things aren't going well in work. It's not my fault, I've just got a bit of a bad habit of doing the wrong thing and landing myself right in it. It's been like that for a while. So when I saw all that good will that bear was getting, I thought, you know, I want to get that as well.

So I did.

I bought myself a bear costume.

It was a good one, I got it online. I could have got something cheaper, but the cheaper ones looked cheap, like, the head bit was just a hood you pulled up that had ears at the top. I wanted the same as that bear I saw at the traffic lights. It cost a king's ransom, but I wanted that kind. That one was perfect, so that's what I got, something that looked like that. I stuck it on and checked myself out in my bedroom mirror, and d'you know what? It was actually better than the one at the traffic lights. It was bigger or something, and it just had a better finish or shine. Maybe it was because the one at the traffic lights was a bit worn out and mine was brand new, I don't know, but it looked really good.

And then I got in my motor, and headed up the toon.

Looking back, maybe I shouldn't have went out on a Saturday night. Maybe a weekday afternoon would have been better. Doing it on a Saturday night was a bit daft, especially when the pubs were just emptying out. But I thought, you know, in at the deep end.

Anyway, it was some buzz. Parking the motor, taking a deep breath, sticking on the big teddy bear head and then stepping out. Right away I heard shouts and whistles and folk beeping their horns as they drove past. That was within ten seconds of stepping out the motor, I'm not joking. And I wasn't even in a busy bit.

When I walked round to Sauchiehall Street, my God! I had lassies running up to me wanting their photo, guys instantly becoming my best mate, I was getting carried, cuddled, it was out of this world. I felt like I was in a boy band. No, I felt like I was all five members of a boy band rolled into one, walking down a busy city-centre street on a Saturday night. I could barely move two steps without somebody else wanting a picture or a cuddle or a handshake or a high five. My jaws were aching with all the smiling I was doing, not that anybody would have seen. I'd only been out in the costume for less than half an hour, yet I was already sure that this was the best night of my life.

Yet how quickly it changed.

It was outside some pizza place a few hours later, when the clubs were starting to empty, when folk really were well and truly wrecked. If I thought I was getting mobbed before, it was nothing compared to now. But nothing too scary, nobody pushing or pulling more than I could handle, just good-natured manhandling, like when footballers congratulate a teammate for scoring, that type of thing. It was a never-ending natural high.

Then a lassie asked me what I was wearing the suit for anyway. I was about to answer, then some guy turned me around for another picture, so I didn't get the chance to reply. Then she asked me again. Out of the whole night, I think she was the only one to ask.

So I told her.

She seemed like a good laugh, a bit mad like me, so I told her.

I told her that it wasn't for anything, it wasn't for charity, nothing like that, I thought I'd just wear it for a laugh. I told her about the person in the bear suit I saw at the traffic lights. I told her the lot. Her expression sort of changed, and she walked away to join her mates. She said something to one of the guys, who leaned closer to her like he didn't quite catch it the first time. She repeated it, then he glanced over to me with a look on his face. His mate saw the look and asked what the problem was, because it was the kind of expression you only had on your face when there was some kind of problem. Then they all glanced over with that very same look.

I started to walk away. I had a bad feeling.

One of them shouted over to me, but I pretended not to hear. Then a few of them came over and stood in my way, and asked me if what the lassie told them was true. They asked me if I bought a bear costume to pretend to raise money for charity. I said that wasn't true, that's not what I told the lassie, and I called her a liar. She told me not to call her a liar, because she told them what I told her, they just got mixed up, they just got that into their heads because they're steaming and weren't listening, so I wasn't to dare call her a fucking liar.

I just started walking away again, but one of the guys booted my arse, and a few people laughed. It was sore as fuck, because I wasn't ready for it, all I could see was straight ahead, no peripheral vision wearing that thing. I kept walking and one of the guys pulled me back, and I could hear a tear in the costume.

One of the guys, steaming, asked me to explain myself. I wasn't paying attention because I was too busy overhearing some of the other guys saying stuff about me to strangers walking by, talking shite, just making stuff up, like that charity thing again, and worse. Just making it up.

I started to walk away once more, this time walking backwards so I could keep my eyes on that lot, and that guy who grabbed me before tried to grab the costume again. So I started to run, because no fucking way I was letting him put another tear in it. Keep in mind how much the thing cost me.

I managed to lose them right away by turning down a wee lane, one of those wee lanes where clubs and restaurants keep their bins, the type of lane where all the guys go for a pish. But as I was about to turn the corner down another lane, I had a look around in time to see them spot where I'd vanished to, and they started coming after me.

I think that kept up for about twenty minutes. Me running down one lane, before turning up another. Me losing them for a while, then being spotted again. I don't know if they were doing it deliberately, I don't know if they were pretending to lose me in order to drag the thing out like a cat-and-mouse thing, but I know that they were enjoying it. Each time I got spotted, they'd toot imaginary bugles and cheer, like they were having a fox hunt. I wasn't enjoying it, personally. I was pretty sure I was running for my life.

But that's me knackered now, so I'm going to stop. I turned around to see if they'd given up, but they haven't. There's around half a dozen of them. I don't know what it is they're going to do, but I'm sure after all this chasing, they're going to make it worth their while. But that's me knackered now.

One of them's doing that bugle sound again, and it's getting another cheer. It's funny. It reminds me of when folk were beeping their horns and cheering at that bear at the traffic lights. God, that seems like ages ago.

Another one of them's just picked something up from the ground. I feel like running again, but that's me done. I really am knackered.

Honestly, these people that run marathons wearing a bear costume.

How do they do it?

FACEBOOK PAST

Sometimes we'd like to go back. Back in time. Back to a happy memory from our past, to relive it for a moment. Or perhaps we'd like to go back to a simpler time in our life, before things got so complicated. Or perhaps we'd like to turn back the clock to a bad decision we made, one that we regret, to make it right and then take it from there. Well . . .

He was on his computer, late at night. Very late. He should have went to bed hours ago, but he couldn't help checking out one last thing, then another, stuff he wasn't even that interested in. He finally ended up on Facebook, which was his cue to call it a night. He had no interest in that at all, so when he found himself there, he knew he really was scraping the bottom of the barrel in terms of ways to avoid going to sleep. And no wonder, the things you'd get on there these days, it was a shambles: the constant game requests to help somebody unlock a level or get a pink ruby or a magic cow; the surprisingly racist posts from people he thought were all right; or the wee People You May Know thing that showed him page after page of people he'd never seen or heard of before. He didn't realise there were that many people he didn't know. Tonight, though, there was one face he did know, very well.

He was about to close the browser when he saw her. She was older now, but he recognised her almost right away, even from the wee thumbnail. Same sort of hair, same colouring. He looked at her name; he didn't recognise it at first because her surname had changed, and her first name was down as Amanda. He'd always known her as Mandy.

He loved her.

He clicked on her picture and went to her profile, hoping that she didn't have all the privacy settings up to the max. But no, everything was there, so he had a nosey. She was married now with a family. There were albums of her on holiday with them, or away to a theme park, or dressing up for Halloween. There were other albums of her on nights out with her mates or taking part in some charity thing or attending somebody's wedding. She was always smiling, smiling that smile that he remembered. She looked so happy and content. He wondered if she would have been that happy and content with him, or he with her. He just wondered, that's all.

He looked through some more of the albums, and then he looked at her posts. Most of them were just wee updates to say she was at some restaurant or bar in

Rutherglen, or to say what she thought of the latest person to get booted off whatever reality programme she was watching, or a link to a donation page to sponsor her for one of her charity things. Nothing that interesting in itself. He yawned and rubbed his eyes, half asleep in his seat, until he spotted something that woke him right back up again. It was a picture. A picture from back in the day. Old pictures like that took you right back, it was a time warp, but this one especially, because he remembered that it was him that took it.

It was taken in Millport, a wee town on Great Cumbrae, an island just off the west coast of Scotland. It was where he first met her, and where he last saw her. It was a place where a lot of families would go for their summer holiday when he was young, families from Glasgow, Paisley, Greenock and thereabouts. The parents would relax and do nothing for a fortnight, while their teenage sons and daughters would meet up with old mates they'd met before, or be introduced to new ones. Like he was with Mandy.

He remembered where it was. Him and a crowd of them were drinking round at the cove, a hideaway from the police near the sea. They were only fifteen, most of them. 'This is my mate Mandy,' somebody said, and he and Mandy shook hands. They had a laugh about how it felt weird when guys shook hands with lassies, it felt like a guy thing, it felt like they should be doing the kissing-on-the-cheek thing like older folk – so they did. A couple of hours later, they were kissing for real at the disco. He told her he really liked her, and she said she liked him as well. He couldn't believe his luck, that somebody like her could like somebody like him.

He woke up the next morning, dreading bumping into her, scared of seeing her pretend that nothing had happened. Later that day, they finally met, when a crowd of his mates met up with a crowd of hers. She smiled that smile at him, and he smiled back. They walked together, and he didn't know what he was supposed to say or how he was to act. She took his hand. He felt fucking light inside when she did that, he felt like he could float away.

A fortnight later most people were heading home, including her. He was fucking gutted, it almost made him feel sick, but he didn't want to show it in case he came across as all clingy. She spent her last day taking pictures with her disposable camera, pictures of her mates, pictures of the cove, before getting one or two pictures of him – it was hard smiling when he knew she was away in twenty minutes. She had one picture left, and asked everybody to get in for a big group photo. He said he'd take it. She said no, she wanted him to come and stand next to him, but he said it was all right, he'd take it. Fuck knows why. Maybe he didn't want a big happy ending, it just didn't feel right, the lot of it felt wrong. He took the photo and walked her round to her house to say goodbye. She offered him her phone number, but he said he didn't think it was best, because she stayed in Rutherglen and that was a good bit away from where he stayed, it wouldn't work out. She shrugged and said, 'Fine,' pretending that she was all right with it, before giving him a cuddle. He walked away, and she walked up the path towards her front door. He turned around to see if she was looking back, if he could get one last look at that smile. She wasn't. And that was the last time he saw her. Until now.

He looked at the group photo on Facebook. There they all were. Ross, Helen, whatshisname, Gregor, Fraser, whatshername, Colin, Carol (or maybe it was Caroline), plus about a dozen more he couldn't quite remember the names of or couldn't quite see. And there, near the middle, was Mandy. He wished he could get a better look. He clicked next, and got just what he was after. It was a copy of the group photo, except she'd cropped it to show just her, and blown it up full size. She filled the screen, her and her smile. That smile, smiling at him, as he took the picture. The smile of summer. He looked at the caption below. 'Happy days', it said. He felt a lump in his throat, and smiled back, before drifting off to sleep.

The following morning he awoke with his head on the desk, as the daylight streamed through the window. He opened his eyes slowly and saw feet standing nearby. He turned around. It was his girlfriend. 'Morning,' he said. But she didn't reply. Instead, she looked at the monitor. He turned to see what she was looking at. It was Mandy.

Or, to put it another way, rather than coming to bed with his girlfriend last night, he apparently chose to fall

asleep looking at a picture of a lassie on Facebook. A
lassie in a bikini top. A lassie that looked no older than
sixteen. And it didn't help matters that she had big tits.

He couldn't help feeling a strong sense of regret. He
wanted to go back. Back before he saw Mandy pop up
in People You May Know. Back before he made the bad
decision to click on her name and end up here.

Back to a simpler time.

Before things got so complicated.

THE INFINITE TEA BAG

He woke up, face down in the dirt of the dusty Nevada desert. He got to his feet and brought his hands to his eyes, to shield them against the midday sun. He couldn't remember passing out. He couldn't remember a thing. But one thing he did know was that he was in trouble. His skin was sunburnt, his head was dizzy, his mouth was as dry as a bone. To his left was an empty road that stretched as far as the eye could see, and the same again to the right. There was nothing out here. Nothing. No signs of life other than the small, dry plants that somehow got by without a drop of water. No snakes, rodents or anything else, dead or alive. No sounds of insects, no cars in the distance, no birds in the sky. Nothing. He didn't know how he got there or how to get out, but he did know that one thing. He was in trouble.

Suddenly, he was hit in the face with a wet tea bag.

It had flown in from the side, smacking him on his cheek, before falling off and landing at his feet. It took a moment for him to realise what had happened. At first, he didn't know he'd been hit, he thought that his skin had simply given in to the sunshine and burst open like a blister. But when he looked down, he understood.

He had been hit in the face with a wet tea bag.

He stared at it, then looked around. He smiled, as if a mate had just chucked it at him at a party, before remembering that he wasn't at a party with his mates. He was in the middle of a desert, with nobody.

What the fuck?

He looked down at the tea bag again and wondered if that's what it really was. Maybe he was looking at some kind of vulture dropping that somehow looked like a tea bag because his eyes were fucked with the sun. But there were no vultures, there were no birds in the sky, and his eyes were fine. He knew what he was looking at. He picked it up for a closer look all the same. No doubt about it: it was a tea bag.

It was a wet tea bag. It was warm, like it had just been used. He gave it a squeeze, and watched the tea dribble down his fingers. He brought it to his nose. It smelled like tea. And after some consideration, he brought his fingers to his mouth and gave them a lick.

It tasted of tea. It was tea.

It was a wet tea bag. Somehow, out here, he had been hit in the face with a wet tea bag.

He looked around again to find out who did it. He wasn't interested in why or how, just who. If he could find a person, all of this would probably make sense soon enough. But nobody was there. There was a wee bush just off the road that could hide somebody, providing they were no taller than a foot. But he wouldn't bother checking that. Maybe later, if he lost his mind.

He looked up, screwing his eyes at the sun. Maybe a bird had dropped it. Maybe a bird had stolen it off a garden table in a nearby town, carried it off all the way here, before looking down to its talons and thinking, Wait a minute, I thought I grabbed a muffin, what the fuck's this? But there weren't any fucking birds, how many times did he need reminding?

He wondered if it was maybe rubbish dropped from a plane. They've got to drop it somewhere. Maybe the tea bag was just the start of it, and any second now it would start raining polystyrene cups and tampons.

But there weren't any planes. Not anywhere. There was nothing in the sky. Nothing. There were astronauts, of course, but let's not go there. Just don't.

Anyway, it came from the side. He remembered it didn't fall from above, it came from the side and hit him right on the cheek, like it was thrown at him full speed from somebody standing ten feet away. But, seeing as nobody was there, the only conclusion was that it was shot. Shot from the distance, from some sort of gun.

You what?

He could feel himself start to go a bit mental, but what else could it be bar a gun? It must have been shot from some kind of sniper rifle. Or a tank.

What, like a tank that shoots tea bags? A tea-bag tank? You're not serious, are you?

He was losing it. He needed to keep it together. A tea-bag tank? No. But maybe something similar. He asked himself again if he was serious, and he had to tell himself to hear himself out and just think about it. Was it not out here they did tests? Military tests? They tested nuclear bombs in places like this, out-of-the-way places; well, maybe now they were testing something more psychological, like hitting terrorists with tea bags so that they freaked out just like he was doing.

Keep it together, mate, keep it together.

He looked back to the bush.

No, don't.

You know nobody could be hiding behind there. That bush couldn't hide a person any taller than twelve inches. Do not fucking look, mate. Don't. If you look behind that bush, you're accepting the possibility that a person of that height came out to the Nevada desert simply to hit you in the face with a wet tea-bag. It would be like pulling a stray thread in your brain. Just fucking leave it.

But he couldn't.

He began walking over, then stopped, in fear of losing his mind. Then he began again, for there was nothing to fear. He would lose his life out here under that sun, he knew it, and the sooner he lost his mind, the better.

He looked slowly around the bush, preparing himself for whatever came next. A fight? Another tea bag?

There was nothing.

He walked all around the bush, he looked inside: nothing. He looked up to the sky once again, he looked down, he looked to the horizon. No birds, planes or tea-bag tanks. There was no explanation for what had happened. None whatsoever.

Unless, of course . . .

Unless this was all . . .

Unless this was all just a . . .

He woke up.

Face down in the dirt of the dusty Nevada desert.

He couldn't remember passing out. He couldn't remember a thing.

NAIL VARNISH

Barry was waiting in the queue in Boots, his stomach in fucking knots. It was his girlfriend Lynn's birthday tomorrow, and he was dreading it. He was dreading it because of what was in his hand. A present. Nail varnish. Was it the right colour? He didn't know, he just did not fucking know, and it was killing him. But he had to make a decision, he had to. The place was shutting and he had to make a decision pronto, he had no other choice, and if it was the wrong colour, well, what was he supposed to do? How was he supposed to know? He just hoped it wasn't the wrong colour, he just hoped it wasn't, but he had to make a decision. He could feel his throat tighten. He took a deep breath; it was only nail varnish. It was only nail varnish.

But it wasn't, was it?

It started with the trainers. The very first present Barry had ever bought Lynn was a pair of trainers. That was back when they just started going out. He didn't really

know what to get, then he spotted a pair of trainers he
liked, so he bought them. Simple as that. That's how
he decided on things back then, that's how simple it was.
She unwrapped the present, looked at her trainers, and
couldn't contain her disappointment. She didn't want
them. They were a decent pair, but she didn't wear
trainers. She thanked him and everything, she was nice
about it, but she told him she would take them back,
and fair enough, he should have known. When had he
ever seen her wearing trainers? Oh well.

   On her next birthday he tried a bit harder. He didn't
want a repeat of the trainers thing, it had made him feel
stupid. He decided he'd get her perfume, but he wouldn't
just get the first thing he saw like he did with the trainers,
he'd spend a bit of time. He smelled about ten perfumes
before deciding on one, then he changed his mind and
decided on another, then he wasn't sure about any of
them. He didn't like that feeling, he wasn't used to it, it
was painful. He eventually picked one that he thought
smelled a bit more elegant than the others, if that's the
term. It smelled classy. He wrapped it up and gave it to
Lynn. As she began unwrapping, Barry felt a tension that
he hadn't felt before. Birthdays were supposed to be fun,
but now it wasn't so much. When all the wrapping was
gone, Lynn looked at the box of perfume, and Barry
could tell by the look on her face that he'd done it again.
Even before she smelled it, he could tell that he'd done
it again. She thanked him, but she said that Vanderbilt
was for old ladies. He'd never heard of it. She said it

smelled like a bingo hall, and laughed. He laughed as well, it was good that she was laughing, that's what he was used to – people made mistakes and people had a laugh. But then she stopped laughing and sighed. Aye, he'd done it again.

Then he did it again, and again. Every year. It got harder, and it took longer, not just longer in terms of deciding what to get, but the tension leading up to the big day, and the aftermath. That got longer. In the early years, he felt pre-birthday tension for as little as a week, and felt shite afterwards for as little as a fortnight. Now, after sixteen years, the pre-birthday tension lasted no shorter than three months, with the aftermath lasting no less than six. That was practically the whole year. It was poisoning him. It was spreading like cancer to every other part of his life. He used to not give a fuck, now every decision felt like he was defusing a bomb, whether it was deciding where to go on holiday or what colour to paint the walls or what socks to wear in the morning. Then there was the big one itself, deciding on what to get her for her birthday. Last year was the worst year yet. It was the straw that broke the camel's back. He'd bought her a hamper. A fucking hamper. A hamper of food off a shopping channel. She asked him if he was joking. He told her he wasn't, and then he broke down in tears.

He couldn't do it any more. He just couldn't. He was already dreading her next birthday. Here, on this birthday, he was already dreading her next. So they came to an arrangement. Lynn said that for her next birthday, they could go out together and she'd just pick what she wanted. It would ruin the surprise, aye, but maybe it was better the surprise was ruined rather than Barry's surprises ruining her birthday. Barry agreed. He felt elated. He felt a weight had been lifted off his shoulders, he felt a sadness leave him that he'd grown so used to that he didn't even realise it was around. It lasted throughout the year, that feeling. His confidence came back, he didn't care what socks he put on in the morning, he didn't even care if they were odd. It lasted throughout the year, right up until a few days ago.

It was that time again. Lynn had mentioned that her birthday was coming up, as if he didn't know. Barry asked her if the deal was still on, if she was going to pick her presents, because that's what she said, that's what she said last year, if she remembered, was that still the case? She told him to relax, it was. So they headed out and into a shop and she picked a dress and a bracelet thing, and he bought it, right there in front of her. It didn't seem right to Barry, it didn't seem how birthday presents should be bought, but at the same time it felt wonderful. They walked out of there arm in arm, and that would have been that. It was perfect, as far as Barry was concerned. But then this morning, the day before her birthday, she had to go and ruin it.

'You know what else I could do with?' she said. 'For my birthday?'

'What?' asked Barry.

'Nail varnish.'

'All right. What colour?'

'You decide.'

'What?' said Barry, not believing his ears.

'You decide,' she said.

Barry felt dizzy. She had asked him to decide. He felt sick. 'But . . .'

'It's only nail varnish,' she said.

But it wasn't, was it?

If he couldn't decide on what colour of nail varnish to get, if he couldn't even decide on that, then he couldn't decide on anything, he couldn't decide full stop. But he had to.

He'd got himself along to Boots, over to the nail varnish aisle, and there he'd stood without moving a muscle for almost ten minutes, gazing at the spectrum of options, at the variety of potential mistakes. He'd picked up a red one and had a look, he was going to get that, but he wondered if that was maybe too 'tarty', so he put it back. He'd picked up a green one, because there was a woman in a wee poster above the nail varnish aisle and her nail varnish was green, and she looked kind of elegant and that reminded him of that elegant perfume he got, the one for old women, and so he put it back. And then he saw Lynn's pal Sandra in there, there in the shop, and she said hello to him as she walked by but he didn't say hello back because his attention was on her nails and they were yellow so he thought that if it was good enough for Sandra then it was good enough for Lynn but then he remembered that Lynn once said that Sandra 'hasn't got a clue', he didn't know what about, but he remembered it was said in a way that meant that Sandra hadn't got a clue in general and therefore that cluelessness would probably also extend to her choice in nail varnish, so he didn't really know what to get, he was going to get blue, he didn't like blue, it reminded him of the blue ice poles that nobody liked when he was young because they were bubblegum flavour and they were minging and although that doesn't relate to the colour of nail varnish he thought he'd go with his gut and put it back because nobody would wear blue nail varnish, he was quite sure of that, then somebody walked by and told him they were shutting so he just shut his eyes and picked one, he just shut his eyes and picked one, and now he was at the counter, the lassie was asking him over to serve him, and he put down the nail varnish but he didn't look to see what colour it was, his attention was on the nail varnish of the lassie serving him, she seemed quite stylish like she knew her stuff yet her nail varnish was blue, and things went a bit blurry at that point and he started to feel dizzy again and sick and he turned and saw Sandra next to him in the queue, she looked concerned, and then he looked back at that blue bugglegum, blue buggle, bubble, blue bubblegum ice pole flavour and he just walked out of there, he just left his purchase sitting on the counter and he just walked out of there,

he started to cross the road outside and he heard a woman shouting to him from behind so he turned around and it was Sandra again and she was waving with one hand and in her other hand was the nailv, nailv, nail vaaarnish and she was shouting something about him leaving something at the till but he couldn't quite hear her for the traffic, then her eyes widened as she pointed to something to his side because he'd forgotten for a moment that he was standing in the middle of the road and something was heading his way, he didn't know what, something big, something casting a big shadow, and he supposed that he'd better make a decision, he'd better decide if he was going to run to this pavement or that, if he was going to run towards this side or that, if he was going to run towards the shop and Sandra with the nail varnish or run to the other side towards Lynn the birthday girl who wants the nail varnish but wasn't going to get any,

he supposed he'd better make that decision pronto because that was a big shadow and it was loud,

he looked at Sandra, at the present, in her hand, at the nail varnish, the one he bought,

he could see what colour it was,

it was quite nice, especially considering he picked it with his eyes shut,

or was it?

he didn't know, he couldn't quite decide,

he wondered what Lynn would have thought,

anyway, as for that decision, that decision that he had to make pronto in relation to being on the road, no, he just couldn't do it any more, he just couldn't,

so he waved back to Sandra from the middle of road,
and smiled.

He'd made a decision after all.

And a pretty big one at that.

JANICE'S FACE

'Janice!' said Tracy, as they were about to pass each other. Tracy had just stepped into the shopping centre as Janice was about to head out.

'All right? How's it going?' said Janice, giving Tracy a kiss and cuddle. 'What you in for?'

'Oh, I'm just taking a top back,' said Tracy, opening her bag to give Janice a glance. 'It's too wee. I didn't try it on at the time.'

'Oh, that's really nice,' said Janice, looking at the top. 'Are you going to get a bigger size or get something else?'

'I might get something else,' said Tracy. 'I've already got a top like it anyway, I don't know why I got it. I think I just fancied grabbing something.'

Janice's scalp began to tear open. It started with a small rip near the top of the head, before extending all the way down to each of her ears. Blood trickled down her forehead and neck.

'Where did you get it?' she asked Tracy. 'New Look?' Her scalp slid forwards slowly towards the front of her face. Her hairline crept down to where her eyebrows used to be, causing her forehead to fold into a flap that rested above the top of her nose like a bulldog.

'Monsoon,' said Tracy.

'Right. D'you know there's a half-price sale on at New Look?' said Janice, her face now hanging inside out off the front of her skull. 'I don't know if you like the stuff in there, but if Monsoon gives you a refund, you could just nip across to New Look. Maybe leave with two tops instead of one!' Her face hung upside down from her chin like a beard.

'That's a good idea,' said Tracy. 'I like some of the stuff in New Look, I'll give that a shot. I'm sure Monsoon will give me a refund, I haven't worn it. Anyway, what about you, what d'you get?'

'Just grabbing a few essentials,' said Janice, saying 'essentials' in a funny voice, in a kind of 'essentials, as they say' way. Her face was red and wet like half a tomato. 'T-shirts for bed, that type of thing.'

'I might grab a few myself,' said Tracy. 'Well, I better get up there before there's nothing left.'

'Good luck,' said Janice, as her face tore away from her chin and dropped on the floor with a slap. 'I hope you nab yourself a bargain!'

'Thanks,' said Tracy, as Janice turned to walk away. 'Oh, by the way . . .'

Janice turned back. 'What?'

Tracy took a step towards Janice, lowering her voice to a whisper. 'Your face fell off.'

Janice touched her skull. She looked at her hands and saw the blood. She looked down and, sure enough, there was her face. She put it back on.

'Thanks,' said Janice, rolling her eyes at herself. She gave Tracy a wave and headed out.

Tracy headed up to Monsoon. They offered her a refund, but she just swapped it for something else, something in Monsoon.

She didn't like New Look.

SEXUAL HEALTH CLINIC

Alec hated coming here. Why the fuck did they have to call it a sexual health clinic? Why did they have to have a big sign above the door that said 'Sexual Health Clinic'? Anybody could see him. Anybody.

'I saw Alec going into that sexual health clinic,' they'd say.

'Are you sure?'

'Of course I'm sure, there was a big sign above the door that said Sexual Health Clinic. That means that Alec's penis has a disease of some kind.'

Could they not change the sign to something else, like 'Caledonian Airlines' or 'Machine Factory'? There were buses that passed here, for fuck's sake, buses full of people who looked out their window to see if they could see anything interesting, people who probably crane their necks when they see that 'Sexual Health Clinic' sign, hoping to spot somebody they know. It would only be a matter of time before that somebody they know was him.

And those were just the problems you faced on the outside, before you stepped through the door. When you got in, there were people everywhere who knew exactly why you were there. A whole waiting room full of them. In a way, though, that wasn't so bad. It was far safer in here than it was out there, not much of a chance of having the finger pointed at you or you being blabbed about. Glass houses and all that.

But despite that feeling of safety, he thought it wouldn't hurt to appear to have less cause for embarrassment than the others. As he passed the waiting room on his way out, he kept his back straight and head held high, as if to say, 'Aye, I've got something, but it isn't as bad as what you've got.' He was sure that everybody else did the same.

'Excuse me, son,' came an elderly voice from the side. 'You there, with the green jacket.' Alec wondered who the fuck was trying to strike up a conversation with him in this place. A neighbour? An uncle? He couldn't imagine anything good coming from it. But it was cool. When he looked around, he saw a sixty-year-old guy in blue overalls, standing outside a 'Staff Only' door. It was the janitor. He opened the door and tapped on the vacuum cleaner at his feet. 'You couldn't give me a hand with this, could you?'

Alec helped the janitor lift the vacuum down a flight of concrete stairs to his wee office in the basement. There was a desk littered with paperwork, and a giant cork-board on the wall pinned with handwritten notes and printouts. Elsewhere was the usual janny sort of stuff, like brushes, ladders, sponges, sprays, screwdrivers, boxes of tools, and general shite lying around that probably came in handy at some point. Alec thought old guys like this had died out long ago, replaced by contracts to cleaning companies or whatever, but somehow this guy had managed to cling on.

'Just over there,' said the janny, pointing to a corner of the room where he had another two or three vacuums on stand by. Alec lifted the vacuum over himself. 'Oh, I remember the days I could do that,' said the janny. 'But it's my back, you see. Sorry.'

'No bother,' said Alec, before plonking it down and heading for the door. 'See you later.'

'I bet you wish you could head out this way, eh?'

'What's that?' asked Alec.

'I'm saying I bet you wish this was the way out, down this way. Under the ground. Like a tunnel, you know?'

Alec smiled. 'Oh right, aye, I get you.'

'D'you know what I mean? Cos this place is a . . . you know? The sign out at that front door. They should have a wee tunnel.'

'Aye, I know what you mean.'

The janny laughed. He had about five teeth. 'That's the good thing about working here. If anybody sees me coming in, they'll just think I'm starting my shift. But for all they know, I've got that fucking AIDS, hahaha!'

Alec nodded, and looked at the door.

'No, I shouldn't laugh, it's must be terrible for you, son. I'm past it, but you're in your prime. The last thing you want is it getting out that you've got something, you know? I'm telling you, a wee tunnel, that would do the trick.'

'Aye,' said Alec, 'but then that wee tunnel would have to have a sign over it instead, so people knew where it went.'

'Oh here, right enough. Fuck, you cannae win, eh?'

'No.' Alec looked at the door. The janny seemed like a nice guy, but probably didn't get much company.

'But they've got to do something,' the old guy went on. 'Because there's a lot to lose. Socially, that is, you know? There's a lot of ignorant people out there, immature people, who would think it was funny to come up to you in front of a lassie you're seeing and tell her about your willy. Tell her what she's in for. Fuck, you wouldn't get your end away for years. Not in this town anyway.'

Alec laughed nervously. 'Don't, mate, you're scaring me. It's fucking terrifying.'

'Oh, don't mean to scare you. I'm just saying that they should take all that seriously, your privacy and whatnot. That sort of thing can ruin your life. But I'll tell you, you want something to be scared of?' The janny typed on an invisible keyboard. 'That's what you should be scared of.'

'Computers?' said Alec.

'Aye, computers. Once a secret gets out on there, Jesus, it's everywhere, just like that,' and he snapped his fingers.

'But that's not the scariest thing. The scariest thing is that that's where all your secrets are kept. That's what they do upstairs, they type all your stuff into their computers, and it all goes off to this one big computer. Can you believe that? It's like telling all your intimate wee secrets to the neighbourhood gossip, and hoping she keeps her mouth shut.'

'Aye, but it's all quite safe and secure and all that, isn't it?' asked Alec. He was beginning to feel vulnerable. Vulnerable enough to be asking an old guy about data security.

'Son, anybody can read about what you've got going on in your pants, if they wanted to. The doctors, the receptionist. Me, even.'

'You could?' asked Alec.

'Aye, anybody could. The police. The papers. Some guy in your work with something against you. And you hear about these leaks, don't you? Mind you . . .'

Alec drifted off a moment. The old guy was right. Every now and then there would be something in the news about another leak, where a hacker group would share the private information of hundreds of thousands of people in a twisted effort to point out the evils of something or other. Sometimes it was bank card details, sometimes it was usernames and passwords. Sooner or later the medical records would surface, presented in a convenient, searchable database for everybody to have fun with on their lunch break.

Genital herpes.

'. . . the stuff on the computers isn't something I worry about myself,' continued the janny. 'I deleted the lot. I just went on when nobody was there and I just deleted the lot. The lot of my stuff, I mean. It's none of their business, that's the way I see it.'

'So you've actually got in and looked at your stuff and . . .'

'Aye, that's what I'm telling you. That's how I know about all this. But don't you fucking tell any of them, son, they'd hand me my jotters. My pension would go up in smoke.'

'I won't tell any of them, don't worry,' said Alec. 'But d'you reckon you could get rid of some of my stuff?'

'Son, I don't want to do anything like that,' said the janny, holding up his hands. 'I told you, if I got caught . . .'

'You won't get caught, just go in and delete it, and that's it done.'

'Well, it isn't as simple as that. I'd have to keep deleting it, wouldn't I? The next time you're here, the doctor would type it back in.'

Alec pulled out his wallet. 'Look, I'll make it worth your while.'

'No, son, put it away, you'll get me fucking jailed.'

'How much?'

'Look, I'll take you back upstairs,' said the janny, about to get out of his seat. 'C'mon.'

'No, how much?' Alec pulled out a handful of notes. The janny sighed and shook his head. He looked at the door, then looked back to Alec. 'I'm gonnae get jailed, I fucking know I am. Fifty quid, I don't know. Gimme fifty.'

Alec handed over fifty quid. The janny stuck it in his pocket, keeping his eyes glued to the door. 'But that's every time. That's fifty quid every time you're in.'

'What?!'

'Forget it then,' said the janny, reaching into his pocket to hand back the cash.

'Right, fifty every time then.'

The janny nodded, then gave Alec a pen and a bit of paper to write down his name and date of birth, and what it was he wanted deleted. Alec scribbled it down fast before the janny had the chance to back out of the deal, then he shook the old guy's hand to set it in stone. Alec headed for the door and looked back to thank the janny, but the janny didn't seem in the mood for good-byes, his head bowed, his eyes shut, and his hands rubbing his temples as he no doubt thought about his pension. But Alec was sure he'd be fine. He hoped so anyway.

When Alec left the front door of the sexual health clinic, his back was straight and his head was held high, except this time it wasn't an act. A bus approached on its way past the clinic, which would usually have Alec practically diving behind a tree. But this time he didn't see the point. He was in the clear. Just check the records if you don't believe him.

And as the day finished at the clinic, the janitor locked

up his office, said goodbye to the receptionist and shuffled out the door.

Where he hopped into his bright red Lamborghini and rolled the fuck out of there.

WELCOME TO THE SHOW

'Ladies and gentlemen,' said Matthew. 'Welcome to the show!'

The sound of applause filled the school gym hall. Parents and teachers clapped their hands. Some of them were smiling, but not all. Most of them weren't smiling. Some were actually scowling, arms folded. There was a bit of history here, you see.

It had taken a lot of convincing to get this show to happen, a lot of convincing. With all the cutbacks at the school, it seemed like a luxury they couldn't afford. The building was falling apart, they were running out of paper, they couldn't even afford a pair of spare shorts for children who had forgotten to bring theirs in for PE, they had to just run about in their trousers.

Morale was low, negativity was rife, people moaned but they knew that nothing would ever change.

Then came Matthew.

His son had recently joined the school at primary two.

They were new to the area. He'd been forced to down-size. The other parents didn't really take to him, they could sense that he wouldn't live in a place like this unless he had to, and that he probably thought he was better than the lot of them. So they grudged this shite. This show. Most of the parents were struggling to put enough money together to buy a school tie, and in comes this airy-fairy posh boy saying that they should all put on a show, a panto type of thing, featuring all the kids. Fuck that, they thought. Fuck that.

But Matthew persisted, putting not only his own repu-tation on the line, but that of his son, knowing full well that his son's popularity in school over the next five years would be in direct proportion to the success of this project. It was risky, but the payoff would be worth it. It would be good for the kids, good for the parents, good for the school. He knew it would cost money, there was no getting around it, they would have to build a stage right there in the sports hall, with the curtains and cables and all of that, and that cost money. But the effect that would have on the school, the joy, the memories, it would be worth every penny.

He stood there on the stage with a smile as the applause subsided and the audience looked on expectantly, awaiting what Matthew had to say next.

Matthew himself waited on what he had to say next.

Matthew's smile faded. It faded as he remembered something. Something he shouldn't have forgotten. Quite a simple thing, really.

He had forgotten to make a show.

No, that can't be right. That can't be right.

He had forgotten to make a show.

A cough from somewhere up the back filled the otherwise silent hall, and then it went silent again.

It had completely slipped his mind. Somewhere in amongst the convincing and door-chapping and jumping through hoops and—

'See, Mummy,' he heard a child say in the audience. 'I told you we weren't doing anything.' Mummy told the child to shut up, don't talk nonsense. It was nonsense, wasn't it? It was going to be a surprise, something like that.

The child looked up to the stage, along with every other child, parent and teacher. All nine hundred of them.

Matthew looked back.

It had completely slipped his mind.

WORKING IN A SUPERMARKET

Tony was stacking the shelves in the wine aisle. They had new bottles just in, expensive ones, about fifteen quid each. He'd better be careful.

'Oops,' said Maureen, his manager, before bumping into him on her way past. Crash! Almost fifty quid's worth of wine on the floor. 'Clumsy,' she said, meaning him, not her. 'That'll be coming out your wages.'

Tony said nothing. He knew what had happened, he didn't imagine it this time. She definitely said 'Oops' before bumping into him. Not after bumping into him, but before. What was going on there? Something about that wasn't right, but he didn't want to jump to conclusions. Maybe she didn't see him until it was too late, maybe that was it. Maybe she realised she was on a collision course but she'd left it too late to move out the way, but not too late to make her apology, in advance, like her mind could respond faster than her body. Maybe that was it. Except it wasn't an apology, was it? And this wasn't the first time it had happened. But that could just mean that she was rude and clumsy, it didn't mean it was deliberate. But it didn't mean that it wasn't. Oh, he didn't know. He just didn't know.

As he headed home that night, he wondered what the fuck had been going on in work these days. Something had changed in there. He'd spoken to a few of his colleagues about it, but they didn't know what he was on about. But something had changed. He didn't know what, he didn't know why.

Like a few weeks ago, he asked if he could do a night shift that Thursday, he told them he could do with the extra cash, but they said no, and that was strange. They used to have to beg him to do the night shift, but now it's a no. Then, the following day, he told them, out of consideration, that if they were thinking of changing their mind and giving him the night shift, it was all right, they were to just forget it, because he remembered that he had a party to go to that night. Know what they did? They came back to him an hour later and told him he'd have to do the night shift after all. He reminded them of the party and that it was for his granny's ninetieth birthday, and quite possibly her last. They told him the world didn't revolve around him and that he should be grateful.

He supposed they were right. But they never used to speak to him like that. Something had changed. He didn't know why.

Then there was that other thing. The thing that'd been happening at the staff entrance. There was a security code they all had to enter on the wee keypad to make the door open. But normally you didn't have to press the buttons because Walter, the security guard guy, would spot you from the inside and press a wee button from behind his desk to open the door for you. Walter would say that he didn't need any machine to tell him that Tony worked there, they knew each other, they had a chit chat practically every morning. But recently, Walter hadn't been doing that, neither the opening of the door nor the chat, none of it. He'd be there behind the desk as Tony approached the door from the outside, but Walter wouldn't look up, even when Tony chapped on the glass. Tony would have to enter the numbers to get in, sometimes getting it wrong and having to spend five minutes digging out the number on his phone. Tony supposed it was maybe an extra security precaution they'd brought in, so that was all right. But quite a few times Tony had spotted other members of staff getting buzzed in by Walter no bother, and they'd get the chit chat as well.

Something had changed. He didn't know what, he didn't know why. Wee things. So many wee things.

At lunchtime he'd look for his milk in the fridge and it would be gone. Or he'd come back from the toilet and his phone would be on the floor, even though he was sure he left it on the table, nowhere near the edge. And when he came home last night, he hung up his jacket and noticed that hanging off the back was a snotter, like somebody had held one of their nostrils shut and blown out the other. A big fucking green slug hanging off the back. It could have been an accident, maybe. Somehow. He just didn't know.

Something had changed. Something had happened, he didn't know what, he didn't know why. He just knew it didn't use to be like this. He sometimes had to remind himself that it never used to be like this. So he got out his remote to do just that. To remind himself. He stuck the telly on, went to his recordings, and played that episode of *The X Factor*. The one he recorded a couple of months ago.

The one he was on.

He didn't get that far in the competition, but far enough that they did a wee feature on him. They brought the film crew round to the supermarket, and there they all were, all the staff, all proud of him, happy for him, all in their T-shirts with Tony's face on the front. It was hard to believe these were the same miserable bastards that he was working with today.

'I've always wanted to sing, singing is my life,' said Tony on the telly.

What had he done? Were they jealous?

'*The X Factor* is my last chance,' said Tony, 'and I need it to work.'

They couldn't be jealous, they were all behind him. They got T-shirts and everything.

'Because I'll tell you something,' he said on the telly, as Tony sat on the couch, wondering where the fuck it all went wrong, wondering why the fuck Maureen kept bumping into him, why Walter wouldn't buzz him in, why there were snotters on his jacket, why his tea smelled of pish, why his bag smelled of farts.

'I'll tell you something,' said Tony on the telly again, shaking his head. 'I don't want to go back to working in a supermarket.'

Oh.

Fuck.

THE TIP

George sat in the back of the taxi, drunk. He was a bad drunk, a nasty drunk. He had this permanent sneer on his face when he got that way, sneering at everything. Sneering at nothing. And now sneering at the driver in the rear-view mirror, even though the guy had done fuck all. He'd actually done George a favour by picking him up, most drivers who saw somebody in that nick would save themselves the likelihood of aggro or having to clean up sick, and just drive on by. But he picked up George, fuck knows why. And did he get a 'thanks', or a 'please' when George told him where to go? No. George just barked out the destination, then proceeded to give the driver hassle for pretty much the whole fucking journey.

'Switch that fucking music off,' he said. The driver switched it off. 'What way are we going, what the fuck's this?' The driver explained that it was the quickest way, and it was. 'Aye right,' said George. 'Roll down the window, it's fucking stinking in here.' The driver told him where the button was to roll the window down. 'You do it. I know you've got buttons next to you to do it, you roll my window down for me, that's what I'm paying you for.' The driver rolled down George's window. George thanked him, sarcastically; it was as close to good manners as the driver was going to get. And when they arrived at George's house, George tutted at the fare. He spent the best part of three minutes counting out the change in his pocket to make sure the driver got not a penny more.

'D'you want a tip, mate?' said George to the taxi driver. 'Don't smoke in bed, hahaha!' He slammed the money into the driver's hand, half of it falling on the floor, before leaving the taxi with the door wide open.

George staggered into his house and straight to bed, straight under the covers. He didn't bother taking his clothes off, he couldn't be arsed. He lay there and thought back to the many people he'd pissed off that night, and laughed. That guy behind the bar. Her in the queue at the chippy. He said something particularly funny tonight, what was it again? He said, 'D'you want a tip? Don't smoke in bed.' He laughed again, that was funny. Who was that to? He remembered: it was the taxi driver. He gave that driver so much shite. George stopped laughing, and thought about that for a second. No, he wasn't thinking of the shite he gave the driver, he didn't regret a thing, he'd just realised that he himself had never actually smoked in bed before. It sounded good. It sounded bad. It sounded like one of those things you weren't supposed to do, like driving without a seatbelt or drinking before midday. It sounded right up his street. He leaned to his side, and grabbed his fags and lighter from his back pocket. Aye, that sounded right up his street.

An hour later, he woke up, screaming, with the room in flames. He pulled the quilt off his face, and the smoke hit his eyes and throat. He could smell singed hair. He covered his face with the quilt again and tried to see how to get out of this, but he could barely see three feet in front of him. He could hear burning, he could hear wood crackling like a bonfire. He grabbed onto the edge of the bed to steady himself, and squealed; the iron bed frame was as hot as a grill. He fell to the floor, cutting his hands on a pint glass that had shattered in the heat. He ran to the door and gripped onto the handle to pull, and had his hand burnt once again. He thought about running back to the bed, but he knew that if he didn't get out of here now, he never would. He braced himself, gripped onto the handle and pulled as hard as he could, but it was no use. The door had expanded in the heat and was jammed shut in the door frame. George pulled his hand away from the handle, leaving some skin from his palm behind. He ran back to the bed, slicing his foot open on the broken pint glass, and dived under the covers. He started shrieking, not just because he was in agony, but because he was terrified. And then he died. It wasn't the smoke that killed him, it was the fire. Burnt. Burnt to death. And it took ages.

As for the taxi driver, that was a different matter. The

funny thing is, the driver usually did smoke in bed, he had done for years. The wife didn't mind it that much, being a smoker herself, but she did think it was a bit dangerous. He assured her, though, that all those warnings were just for alkies who lived by themselves, people so wrecked that they could start a fag but couldn't stay conscious for long enough to finish it. When had he ever done that? Never. Mind you, he'd never been this knackered, not for a long time anyway; three shifts, back to back. Christ, the way he let that wee ballsack in the back seat talk to him tonight showed him just how knackered he was. Usually he'd have pulled the handbrake on a guy like that and dragged him out by the throat. But tonight he didn't bother, he couldn't be arsed.

He thought about that for a second. No, not how knackered he was – he was still going to have his fag – he was thinking about what that guy had said. His wee parting shot, what was it again? Something about a tip. He couldn't quite remember, but it was something . . . about . . . a . . .

The driver woke up in the morning with his two wee daughters jumping up and down on the bed, and he gave them a cuddle. When they were gone, he stretched, then turned to the bedside table to get his fags for a morning smoke. His fags weren't there. He was about to run after his daughters, thinking they'd grabbed the packet when he wasn't looking. But then he remembered the fags weren't there because he hadn't taken them out of his jacket pocket the night before, because he didn't have his bedtime fag. Now there was a turn-up for the books. He thought about getting up and heading to the cupboard for his jacket, but the idea wasn't as appealing as lying all cosied up under the covers, especially after the shift he'd put in yesterday.

It wasn't until later in the day that he realised he hadn't smoked in twenty-four hours. One of his daughters said something about fresh air. And that was that. Him and his wife both decided to knock it on the head, and other than a few blips along the way, they never went back. The driver added an extra ten good years onto his life that would have otherwise been snatched off him by cancer. He started going swimming, jogging and playing five-a-sides. And he didn't stop telling everybody that he felt fucking marvellous these days.

As opposed to George.

George was toast.

What was it he said again? 'D'you want a tip, mate? Don't smoke in bed, hahaha.'

Fucking backfired, that one, didn't it?

MR NORMAL

There once was a guy. A normal guy. I don't quite know how to describe him. He was a normal guy with normal hair, a normal build and normal clothes. And his face was, well, it was just sort of normal. You might think I'm not trying hard enough to describe how this man was, you might think that I'm failing as a writer, but if you saw him yourself, you'd say the exact same thing. Normal. A normal sort of guy.

He was the sort of guy whose name you'd never remember, even if you were introduced to him dozens of times over the course of a night. He could be on your train every morning as you went to work, sitting right there in front of you, every day for a year, yet you wouldn't know him from Adam if he came up and shook your hand in a pub. He's that one in your primary school class photo you don't recognise, even though he was in every class you ever had.

He was the sort of guy that you wouldn't look at

twice if you saw him walking down the street. You'd see him, you'd think 'person', then look at something more interesting instead, like the pavement. Even when you looked at him, the chances are you weren't really looking at him at all; you were looking through him, the way you'd look through the wallpaper of a waiting room. A mere glance at him would make you think of something else, to occupy your mind during the vacuum that his appearance had created. Perhaps your mind might decide not to see him at all. It might pick him up in your peripheral vision, determine from his normal shape and normal average colour of clothes that he was of no interest whatsoever, and tell you not to bother looking, that it simply wasn't worth even a second of your time.

In fact, he was so normal that he could probably walk straight into a bank, his face in plain sight, and rob the joint of every penny without fear of being caught. It wouldn't be because the police would have trouble finding a robber described as 'normal', although that would be trouble enough. It would be because nobody would see him do it. The security guard wouldn't see him walk past towards the safe; the cashiers wouldn't see him lift the money from the till right under their noses; the customers wouldn't see him remove their purses and wallets and watches and rings right out their hands.

And funnily enough, here he was. In a bank.

To rob it?

No.
To pay a bill. Just to pay a bill.
See, I told you.
Mr fucking Normal.

THE GOAT

One night a man had a wee bit too much to drink. His friends told him it would be best if he left the pub and went home to his wife. They meant it in a nice way, they knew he was in a bad place right now, and he was making a fool of himself. After all, he wasn't just some lad in his twenties, he was fifty-two, and a good father.

He left, and soon got lost. He ended up walking down some country road in the dark.

He saw a dead goat trapped in a barbed-wire fence.

He shagged it.

THE COUCH

Davie was watching the telly on his couch when he felt something move. He got off his couch, turned around and noticed that his couch had come to life.

'Feed me,' it said.

For a second Davie did nothing. Then he walked calmly towards the living-room door. He was going to arrange an appointment with a doctor, he had a feeling he might have a brain tumour or something. But the couch moved quickly to block his path.

'Feed me,' it said again.

Davie could smell the couch's breath. It smelled of raw mince, it smelled like a butcher's. No, this was no illusion, not with that breath. This was real.

'What do you want to eat?' asked Davie. 'Biscuits? Cornflakes?'

'No,' said the couch. 'People. Feed me people.'

Davie shook his head. 'I can't do that. I can't.'

'You can, and you will,' said the couch. 'Or else!'

'Or else what?' asked Davie, taking a step back.

'Or else I'll never let you sit on me again!'

Davie imagined what it would be like watching the telly without a couch. He remembered having to do it once after he had his mate Frank over to watch the football. They had a few drinks, Davie let Frank crash on the couch, and the next morning Davie woke to find the couch was soaked in lager and Frank had fucked off without a word of explanation. Two days it took for the thing to dry. It said you weren't to put the covers in the dryer, so he had to just let it dry in by itself. Two days. Two days without a couch. The only other option he had was this bolt-upright seat that always done his back in, or lying on the deck with his hip bone or elbow or something else digging right into the laminate flooring. It wasn't exactly comfy.

'All right,' said Davie. 'I'll do it.' And he headed out.

It didn't take him long to decide on who to bring back. It was Frank, of course. He told Frank it was some laugh that, last time he came round, and that they should do it again. They should just forget about that thing that happened, put it behind them, just get the booze in, get the football on, and just crash out on the couch. That sounds good, doesn't it? Frank could just crash out on the couch, just like last time. The second they get back to Davie's, Frank could just lie on the couch, the whole thing to himself, and crash there for the night. Crash on the couch.

'All right,' said Frank. 'I get the message. I can crash on your couch. Thanks.'

They got back, took off their jackets and turned on the telly. The football had already started. A penalty. A penalty in the first five minutes. Frank stood watching, his eyes glued to the screen. He sparked open one of the cans and picked up a pint glass from the table. Davie gestured towards the couch. Frank stepped over to the couch, his eyes never leaving the penalty. He began crouching down slowly as he poured the lager into the glass. The referee whistled for the player to take the kick. The player ran up, Frank sat down and the couch opened wide. It opened up like a gaping arse with the teeth of a shark. Crunch! Gnash, gnash, gnash! Gnash, gnash, gnash, gnash, gnash, gnash, gnash!

And that was the last time Frank went round to Davie's.

He knew Davie had a brain tumour and everything, but he'd had enough of this pillow fight thing or whatever the fuck it was, every fucking time he went over, every time he sat on that couch.

Lager fucking everywhere. He was soaked.

Plus he missed that fucking penalty.

I'LL LET YOU GO

So I'm walking up the road and I bump into somebody I know and we stop and chat. He talks a bit, I talk a bit, and we're back and forth like that for a minute or two until he finally says, 'Listen, I'll let you go.'

He'll let me go.

I know what that means.

I'm not stupid.

It means that he thinks he's got somewhere better to be and I don't. It means he thinks he's so busy with places to go and people to meet but I'm some sort of sad-case loner that has nowhere to go and nobody to meet and I just want to spend all my time talking to anybody who'll have me, like I'm one of these folk you see standing up the front of the bus talking to the driver. That's what that means. That's what he thinks. But he doesn't want me to know that that's what he thinks in case it hurts my wee feelings, so he's making out that in fact it's the other way about and that I'm actually the one with important business and he doesn't want to take up another moment of my precious time, so he'll let me go, he'll kindly let me go.

No no. No, I'll let him go.

But I can't. He's just let me go, he's just finished the conversation, you can't tell somebody you don't have time for this conversation when the conversation's done.

So I start up a new one.

I ask him where he's staying these days, as a kind of by-the-by, and he tells me he's staying in roughly the same bit, but in a nicer house. I ask him to describe the house to me, and he does. Then I ask him if he ever bumps into any of the old faces that we used to hang about with. He tells me about one or two that he's seen, and about halfway in, I decide to look at the time on my phone then look up the street at an imaginary place I need to go. When he's finished, I say, 'All right, that's good. Well, listen, I'll let you go.'

And guess what he says. He says, 'All right, bye.'

I know what that means.

I'm not stupid.

It means that he thinks that, unlike me, he hasn't got time to play silly wee mind games. It means that if I think I've won this wee battle, he's happy to let it slide, because he's too busy to care, he's got bigger fish to fry. Even though it was him who started it. Even though I wouldn't be standing here playing his silly wee mind games if it wasn't for him fucking starting it, and now that he lost he's going to bail out and try to kid himself on that he's the big grown-up with the pure big busy fucking schedule. That's what that means.

And now he's going to tell everybody. He's going to tell everybody that I just wander about with nothing to do and that you should cross the road when you see me, like I'm some sort of fucking screwball.

No, no. Can't have that.

So I try to hook him back in, I ask him, 'By the way . . .' but he says he has to go. I say, 'No wait, it's just one wee thing,' and he says he doesn't want to be late. I say, 'No, listen,' and he says, 'What?'

And I ask him, 'Has your house got a garden?'

But before he has a chance to answer, I run. I run like a whippet. I run faster than I've ran in the last twenty-five years. I don't think I've run that fast since secondary school. I run so fast I can't hear his answer because of the wind in my ears, it's like I'm on a bike.

So he can tell whoever he wants about me, tell whoever he wants whatever he wants, tell them a pack of lies for all I care. And the same goes for you.

Because I don't care. I don't care at all.

I've got shit to get on with. A lot of people want to talk to me right now and I've got a lot of things to do. And all of it is important and critical as fuck.

So listen, if you don't mind . . .

I'll let you go.

ROOM WITHOUT A ROOF

Jason didn't know how to go about it, so he went into the Citizens Advice Bureau to ask. He wanted to know if he needed some kind of planning permission thing for what he was about to do. He hoped not, because he didn't want to have to wait, he wanted to do this now. But he asked anyway.

He explained that he'd not been feeling too happy recently; he'd been feeling a bit down in the dumps. He'd stick on the telly to watch something funny to cheer him up, but it'd never raise a smile. He thought about meeting up with some mates to see how they were doing, but he couldn't give a fuck. And last night he treated himself to a bubble bath, he actually went into a shop to get some bubble bath, and he used it last night, he had himself a bubble bath, and waited, waited to be happy, until his fingers were all wrinkly and the water went cold.

Nothing.

So that was it. He'd tried everything. So while he was there in the bath, he thought he may as well top himself.

He got out, plugged his radio into the socket in the hall and carried it back into the toilet. He got in the bath, holding the radio above the water, and switched it on. He was just about to drop it in and be done with it all, but on came that song. That happy song. The one about being happy, by Pharrell. That one.

Jason told the Citizens Advice guy that he lay there in the bath, listening to Pharrell singing about how happy he was, much happier than Jason. He wondered how the fuck anybody could be that happy, he wondered how you got that happy, that way Pharrell was singing in the song. Singing about not having a care. Singing about being a hot air balloon. But it was that bit where he sang about 'a room without a roof', that's what really got him wondering. 'Clap along if you feel like a room without a roof'. Jason didn't get it, he didn't know what was so happy about that, about 'a room without a roof'. Maybe it's because it lets in more natural light, or maybe it's because it feels good to sleep under the stars, like when you go camping. He just didn't know. But he was going to give it a try.

The Citizens Advice guy asked him to clarify just what it was he was going to try. Jason said that he knew what the guy was going to say, that he was going to ask Jason about the rain, what if it started raining, but Jason said he'd cross that bridge when he came to it. The Citizens Advice guy still wasn't sure what Jason was saying. Jason said he wanted permission to remove the roof from his house. The guy asked Jason if he was serious. Jason said he was deadly serious, mate, deadly serious, he had to give it a shot, he'd tried everything else, bubble bath, the lot. The Citizens Advice guy asked some questions about Jason's property out of politeness, even though he knew Jason had fucking no chance. Jason said it would be cool, he lived in a flat, but it was a top-floor flat; he was sure his neighbours wouldn't mind. The Citizens Advice guy tried not to laugh. When Jason pointed out it wasn't even his flat and that he was renting it off the council, the Citizens Advice guy couldn't hold it in any longer, he laughed Jason out of there. He felt bad for doing it, but for crying out loud.

Jason went ahead and did it anyway. It was either that or he was topping himself, no two ways about it, and he didn't need permission to make that decision, not from anybody. So he climbed out of his living-room window, up the drainpipe and onto the roof. Some people in the flats across the road saw him and thought he was a thief stealing tiles, and they phoned the police.

The police took Jason to the station and let him off with a caution, but as soon as Jason got back home he went right back onto the roof and started tearing tiles off like he was the Hulk. When one of the tiles smashed onto the roof of a passing motor, the police were phoned again, and this time the judge had no option but to give Jason a custodial sentence.

He had a lot of time to think. He had a lot of time

to think not only about his actions, but about that song. The song that inspired his actions. What the fuck was Pharrell on about? His attempt to have a room without a roof hadn't brought him happiness, it had landed him in the fucking jail.

And then it clicked.

'Clap along if you feel like a room without a roof', that's what Pharrell said. Maybe what he was saying was a room without a roof is actually shite, so if you feel like that, if you feel shite, clap along, it'll cheer you up.

Outside the cell, one of the prison staff responsible for Jason's twenty-four-hour suicide watch took a look through the peephole.

He saw Jason clapping, and smiling.

It was a fucking shame for that boy, it really was. He shouldn't be in here, caged like an animal, there was obviously something wrong with him.

Mind you, he did look kind of . . . happy.

THE MAGNET

Brian stood at his cooker, boiling an egg. Just the one. It was all he had left, and it fucked everything up. The timing.

All he wanted was a soft-boiled egg. A soft-boiled egg. But it was never right. Well, it was sometimes right, but he wanted it right every time. If it's only right some of the time then it's never right, it's wrong. The recipe, that is. Five minutes, they say. Five minutes. But it isn't as simple as that, is it? Depends if you start from hot or cold water. If it's from cold, how cold? If it's hot, how hot? Boiling? What about the size of the pot? How much water do you stick in? And what if the pot only contained one egg, like now, rather than three or four? What then? Did anybody know?

Maybe it was just four minutes, actually.

Just then a man from the future appeared, right out of thin air. It was Brian. Another Brian. A Brian from the future.

They looked at each other for a bit, not sure who should speak first. Future Brian decided that since he was the one who had appeared out of nowhere, he should try to explain himself.

'I'm from the future, I think,' said Future Brian.

Normal Brian looked him up and down. Future Brian didn't look from the future. He didn't have a hoverboard or a visor. He didn't look like he came from the year 5000. He looked more like he came from five minutes from now. And as it turned out, he did.

'I was boiling an egg,' said Future Brian. 'That egg. Just trying to work it out, the timing and everything. And then that magnet fell in the water.'

They both looked at the wee magnetic picture frame that was on the steel extractor fan above the pan. It had a picture of Brian and his ex-girlfriend. The steam from the pan was steaming up the steel, making the frame slide slowly down the extractor fan, towards the edge.

'So what you're saying is . . . ?' asked Normal Brian.

'Aye,' said Future Brian.

'Boiling a magnet turns back time,' they both said in unison.

And for a while, they said nothing. They just stared at each other. It was quite a lot to take in.

'What d'you want to do?' asked Future Brian.

'We could, um . . .' Normal Brian had a think. 'We could . . . I don't know. Go back to the dinosaurs or something.'

'No,' said Future Brian. 'How would we get back? Back to here, back to now? And how do we get that far back in time in the first place? Dinosaurs? What you on about?'

'Aye, all right,' said Normal Brian.

They had a think.

'Can we go into the future?' asked Normal Brian.

'How would I know?' said Future Brian.

'Because if we could, we could maybe, I don't know. We could . . . I don't know.'

'Deary me,' said Future Brian.

'You're putting me on the fucking spot,' said Normal Brian. 'You come up with something.'

Normal Brian wondered why Future Brian was such a dick. He wondered if coming from the future made you less patient, like you don't have the time for any jibber jabber, because coming from the future meant you had less time left in your life. Or maybe it meant you had more time, and it was boring because you had to relive everything again. Either way, Normal Brian had better come up with something before Future Brian lost it.

'Look,' said Normal Brian. 'Maybe we should forget about the past and future and think about the present.'

Future Brian didn't know what he meant.

'Like, what can we do right now, me and you?' Normal Brian continued.

They wondered.

'What can me and you do,' said Normal Brian, 'that's

only possible because there's two of us? Something we maybe couldn't or wouldn't do with somebody else.'

They wondered. And then wondered some more. Normal Brian looked out the window, as if he'd find the answer out there.

Then he felt Future Brian hold his hand.

Normal Brian looked at Future Brian's hand, and then his face. Future Brian's cheeks were slightly flushed, his mouth was parted and he had a hard-on. To Normal Brian's surprise, it started to give him a hard-on as well. Normal Brian began to squeeze Future Brian's knob through his tight jeans, as Future Brian went in for the kill, unzipping Normal Brian's jeans and gently coaxing out Normal Brian's stiff, veiny prick.

Just as things were about to get hot and nasty, another man from the future appeared and broke it up. It was another Brian. This one was from a slightly more distant future than Future Brian, about another five minutes.

'Stop it, stop that right now,' said Distant Future Brian, shoving Normal Brian's cock back into his jeans. If anybody else did that, thought Normal Brian, if anybody else grabbed his cock and shoved it back in his jeans like that, they'd get their jaw cracked. But somehow this other Brian doing it made it all right. It was all their cock after all.

'You better have a good reason for this, mate,' said Future Brian to Distant Future Brian, his hard-on losing steam.

'It didn't work out,' said Distant Future Brian. 'Let's

just leave it there.' Future Brian was about to ask Distant Future Brian to go into more detail, but there was a certain look in his eyes, a certain experience, that told him all he needed to know.

'Anyway, we had a better idea,' said Distant Future Brian. 'Listen up.'

And he went on to describe an elaborate plan to get rich. Filthy rich.

'A casino!' said Normal Brian. 'Of course! Why did I not—'

'Fucking shut up and listen,' said Distant Future Brian. Normal Brian noted that Distant Future Brian was even less patient than Future Brian. It looked like his theory was right, whatever that was. He thought he'd better fucking shut up and listen before he had the pair of them at him.

The idea involved one of them playing roulette, another one of them standing nearby and taking note of the numbers as they came in, and then that one telling those numbers to the third one. That third one would be ready to do the magnet-boiling thing in the toilet cubicle, and he'd do that by using one of those wee gas camping stove things that he'd have to smuggle into the casino under a big raincoat along with a pot of water and a magnet. Simple as that.

'Simple as that,' said Normal Brian sarcastically. 'Fucking what?'

They argued. Their argument led to a fight. And their fight, inevitably, led to more hard-ons.

Just then a man from the future appeared. Another Brian. Fuck this. Seriously, fuck this. There would be no stopping the cocks this time around, just let him try. But then the three Brians saw what was in the hands of this last and Final Brian. Poly bags, stuffed full of notes. £353,890 worth of notes, to be precise.

'It worked!' cried Normal Brian, clawing at the bags. 'It worked!'

'Hold on,' said Future Brian, pushing Normal Brian back. 'It's not all yours, mate.'

'He never said it was,' said Distant Future Brian. 'It belongs to all of us.'

'Aye,' said Normal Brian, reaching for the bags again. 'In fact, I should get most of it. Yous wouldn't be here if it wasn't for me.'

'Don't talk shite,' said Future Brian, slapping Normal Brian's hand out the way. 'It was me that told you about boiling the magnet, I should get the most. Half, at least.'

'Sorry, whose fucking idea was the casino?' asked Distant Future Brian, barging between them both.

'You said "we" had the idea,' replied Future Brian. 'You said "we". Why are you making out it was just you? Why are you lying? Why are you lying? Why are you—'

Final Brian raised his hands slowly and smiled.

'Easy, lads, easy,' he said. 'You don't have to worry about any of that. Not one bit.'

'How come?' asked Normal Brian. Then he noticed something. 'Wait a minute,' he said. 'Where are the others?'

'Aye,' said Future Brian. 'Where are they? How come you've got all the money?'

'Maybe that isn't all the money,' wondered Distant Future Brian. 'Am I right?'

Final Brian reached down into one of the cupboards. 'The answer, boys,' he said, 'is right here.'

He brought out a large cast-iron pot.

'Iron,' said Normal Brian, starting to get it. 'Magnets are attracted to iron. Whereas the other pot . . .'

'Is just steel,' said Future Brian.

The three Brians turned to look into the steel pot on the gas and the boiling magnet within, as Final Brian carried the iron pot over from the cupboard.

'I see, so if we were to boil a magnet in an iron pot,' theorised Distant Future Brian, before going blank. 'Em . . . what would that do? Sorry.'

'Aye,' said Future Brian. 'What can an iron pot do that this one can't?'

'It can do this,' said Final Brian behind them, before bashing in their skulls.

As they lay there with the tops of their heads cracked open, Final Brian was reminded of something. The egg! The egg, of course, oh my God, he nearly forgot.

He fished it out the water and stuck it in an egg cup next to some toast and a cup of tea. He sliced the top off with his teaspoon and looked inside.

It was perfect.

Absolutely perfect!

THE TIGHT LACES

He was to put together this pitch. They asked him last week. He was to put together this pitch, this presentation, type the thing up, get it rehearsed and present the thing to the client tomorrow. He asked his bosses if he could work from home; it just helped him be more cre-ative. They preferred it if he did it in the office, so they could see how it was going, but he insisted, and they said OK. That was a week now, that was a week he'd been working on it. He was to send it off to his bosses by 5 p.m. today, and then, pending their approval, he'd present the thing tomorrow. A big job. A big, big job. Very important. And he hadn't written a thing.

It was just the pressure. It was a lot of pressure, and that sort of thing got in the way of creativity, it got in the way of ideas. So he took it easy for the first few days. In other words, he did nothing. When he finally got started, he just couldn't do it, he just wasn't feeling it. It was that blank screen staring back at you, so many options, it was like looking at a menu with too many things on it, it made it so hard just to go for it. He felt he needed to loosen up, so last night he got hammered.

He woke up at 11 a.m. this morning. Only six hours left. There were emails waiting for him, missed calls. He texted back to assure his bosses he was on it, he'd have it to them by 5 p.m., as promised. He switched on his laptop and stared at the screen, that big white screen, until 1 p.m. He'd had no breakfast, no shower. He decided to head to a cafe, he'd take the laptop, he just needed out the house, that was it. A change of scenery.

He sat in the cafe, staring at the screen. He checked the time – it was just after two. Less than three hours left. He put his hands on the keyboard. He was going to get started. He was just about to get started. Any time now, he'd start typing and get started. There was just one problem.

His laces were too tight.

It sounds like a trivial problem, but it was quite annoying. It was a niggling wee thing, like a pea under a hundred mattresses. It was the lace on his right shoe; he'd tied it too tight when he rushed to get out the house. It felt like the tongue of his shoe was pressed against the veins in his foot, like it was cutting off the blood flow, he wasn't sure, but it was just this wee nuisance that he really didn't want right now. He wasn't blaming it for the fact that he hadn't typed anything, he'd had all week to do that, but he thought he should sort them out before he got cracking.

He bent over and poked his head under the cafe table, and untied the lace on his right shoe. He gave the rest of the lace a tug here and there to loosen it all up. Ahhh, that felt better. Much better. He could get started now.

It was quite nice down there, he thought. It was a wee booth he was in, not a lot of light getting under the table. It was quite nice, nice and dark. Not like up there, up there on the table where the laptop was, with that screen. That big, bright white screen, that big, bright white light shining in your face. It was better down below. It was a welcome break. You needed a break, a break from that light, it's bad for your eyes, that. Looking into screens for too long can be bad for you.

Maybe he should stay down there for a wee bit longer. What's the rush? Can a man not duck under a table to loosen his laces and then maybe stay a while? Does everything have to be done on time and done with determination, must you always do what you say you were going to do? Why must we rush to get something done if it's only to move onto something else immediately after? Can a man not just linger in the gaps between?

Two hours he stayed under there.

They had to phone the police.

THE SIZE OF SALLY

There was something up with Sally, she wasn't feeling too well. She felt sluggish and stiff, she felt heavy, and that wasn't right, not for somebody like her, somebody who kept herself fit and active. Yet she felt like an old woman. An old woman who smokes sixty a day and eats burgers for breakfast.

She went to the doctor, and right away he could tell something was up, so much so that when she walked into the room, he sprung out his chair to help her get to her seat. She was in a bad way. When she sat down, he asked her if she'd been getting enough exercise. She told him that wasn't it. He asked if she smoked or liked a drink or whatever. She shook her head. He asked her if she'd been feeling down, if there had been a bereavement, if she was prone to mood swings. She said it was none of that, it was nothing she could explain; she'd looked it all up on the NHS site and forums and everything else, there was just no explanation, there weren't any lumps, there wasn't any pain, the stiffness wasn't in any one place, it was all over. She was starting to lose her patience. And then she collapsed.

The doctor phoned an ambulance and she was rushed to hospital, where they prodded and poked and did some scans. There appeared to be something wrong with the scanning machine, it was giving some strange results, so they did another round. But it was the same thing. That couldn't be right, it couldn't be. They scanned somebody else; they were fine. Then another; they were fine as well. Then they scanned Sally once more, but there were those strange, strange results yet again. Sally's heart monitor started going haywire. They were going to have to operate.

The surgeon started with one of her fingers, somewhere inconspicuous, a small cut at the end of her left thumb. He was reluctant to jump in head first with a slice right down her belly, regardless of what the scans said, because the scans defied belief. He just wanted a peek. He pulled the skin apart at the cut, and saw that the scans were right. Dear God! He cut open the rest of her fingers, then her arms, then everything. He cut her open like a teddy bear being torn apart at the seams, and revealed what was inside.

It was Sally!

Inside Sally was Sally, another Sally. It was like the inner Sally had been wearing an outside Sally as some kind of Sally suit. But now it was gone, and she woke up feeling refreshed and reinvigorated, back to her old self, albeit a wee bit smaller. They peeled away the rest of her skin, got her all cleaned up, and then they asked her what she wanted to be called. She couldn't keep her old name; she was a new person in effect, the computer wouldn't allow it. She liked her name, though, so she said, 'I know. Call me Sally 2.'

Sally 2 walked out the hospital and right back into her life, feeling better than ever. Faster. Lighter. After a month or two, she began to slow down, but she put that down to her body just settling in. Then not long after that, she started to feel even slower. Sluggish and stiff, heavy, until she didn't feel too well at all. Then she collapsed. An ambulance was phoned, and back to the hospital she came for some more prodding and poking and another few scans, only this time there was no hesitation. She was wheeled to the operating theatre as quick as a flash, where the surgeon cut her from head to toe with one big swoosh of the knife like she was a box of flat-pack furniture. And inside Sally 2 was, you guessed it, another Sally. Sally 3.

Sally 3 was smaller again, but identical in every other way. She woke up, refreshed and reinvigorated, before getting cleaned up, dressed, and walking right out of there, feeling even better than before. Two weeks later she was back, and out popped an even smaller Sally 4.

Sally 4 walked right out of there, before collapsing in the hospital car park. Back she came, and out popped Sally 5, who collapsed right there on the bed.

Sally 6 was fine, though, for the best part of a year.

But then she died. She was taken to the morgue, where they cut her open for a post-mortem, only to find Sally 7. Dead. They cut her open, only to find Sally 8, also dead. So was Sally 9. But when they cut her open, to their surprise, out popped Sally 10, refreshed and re-invigorated and all raring to go. All two foot of her.

But then she died.

They decided to bury Sally 10, to put her out the misery of this Russian doll carry-on, to let the woman have some peace, for heaven's sake. Plus it was a nice round number. So they put her in a coffin and stuck her in the ground.

Some years passed, with no mention of Sally 1–10, but after a while, people began to talk. They began to wonder. Sally 10 was dead, yes, but what about Sally 11? Or Sally 12? What had they done? And what would they find? So out came the shovels, and the coffin was dug up. As curious as they were, nobody was in any rush to be the one to open it. The surgeon stepped forward, and quite rightly. He leaned down and pulled off the lid, then stood aghast at what was inside.

The coffin was full to the brim with layer upon layer of dried-up Sally skin. It was like puff pastry. It looked like all that crumpled paper you get inside a shoe box. Except there were no shoes. And no Sally.

Sally was gone.

They cleaned out the coffin carefully, looking for what might be a wee Sally 15, or a tiny Sally 30, or a minus-cule Sally 100. They couldn't find her. Not even with a microscope. Not even with the best microscope in the world.

But she was there.

Sally 1,000? Higher.

Sally 1,000,000? Much higher.

Sally a billion billion?

Even higher than that. And, therefore, even smaller.

So small that she had slipped between the fibres of the coffin. Then she slipped into the space between the atoms. And then she slipped between space itself.

So small that she slipped between hours, minutes and seconds. She slipped between the smallest definition of a moment. She slipped between time.

She was so small that she slipped between knowledge. Infinitesimally small. She slipped between and beyond understanding itself.

Now, think for a moment about how small that is. Try and wrap your head around something so small, can you do it?

Well, see that size?

That's yer da's cock.

A SIMPLE MISTAKE

It was a simple mistake, but a deadly one. He knew the rules.

If you gave them any reason to believe you weren't cut out for the job, they had to let you go. If you gave them any indication that you were a liability rather than an asset, they had to let you go. With immediate effect.

It really was such a simple mistake, but he could understand their concerns. He had his finger on the big red button, after all. He knew the launch codes. If communication was lost or the General was incapacitated in some way and a decision had to be made, then he'd be the one to make it. You couldn't have somebody in that position making mistakes like this. Not just on the field, but here at home. Not even right here in his own home. And they were watching. He knew the rules. They had to let him go. That's how they put it when he took the position. If anything like this should arise, 'we'd have to let you go'. He knew what that meant.

It was understandable. He wasn't just some pencil-pushing office worker. They couldn't just ask him to clear his desk and show him the door. Not with his knowledge. Not with what he knew. Why, he'd walk right out and right into the wrong hands.

And they couldn't just place him on an island somewhere to live out the rest of his days. The other side would stop at nothing to find him and promise him the world. Promise him a bigger island. And all he would have to do is tell them a secret or two.

No, they couldn't do that, but neither could they keep him. Not after a mistake like this. Such a simple mistake, but so revealing. Repeat a mistake like that on the field and, well, it would cost the lives of billions. Perhaps the world entire.

He took a moment to reflect upon his life, in the remaining few moments before it would come to an end. He looked at the box of cereal in his hand, the one he got up for in the middle of the night, the contents of which he'd just poured into a bowl because he was feeling peckish.

And as the sniper bullet pinged through his kitchen window towards his head, he couldn't help feeling a bit silly. Well, it was silly, taking the cereal out the cupboard and the milk out the fridge, then, when done, walking to the fridge to put the milk back, opening the door, wondering for a moment why the milk won't fit back in, then realising it's because you're not holding the milk, you're holding the box of fucking cereal instead. That was silly.

Yet such a simple mistake.

But he understood their concerns.

BUTTERFLY

Louise was walking through the park with her mate. What a day, sunny with a light breeze. And this bit of the park was lovely, a wee quiet bit, all peaceful and tranquil. She smiled, and was just about to say to her mate how beautiful everything was when she saw something that put the cherry on top.

'Look, a butterfly!' said Louise, as it landed on a leaf. She whipped out her phone to get a snap, but the thing flew off. 'Awww,' she said, 'I think I scared it.' She watched as it fluttered away, this way and that, before doubling back. 'Where's it going?' she asked. She laughed as it hovered around her head for a while, before landing right on her nose.

'Oh. My. God,' she said quietly, not wanting to scare it away a second time. She reached for her phone slowly; she didn't want any sudden movements to fuck this up. This was definitely going to be her profile pic, for a very long time.

'Don't move. I've got it,' said her mate, pulling out her phone instead.

'Thanks.'

Louise began breathing as slowly as she could to stay calm and still. She was almost more nervous than this tiny wee thing on the end of her nose. 'This will probably make me sound really stupid,' she whispered, 'but butterflies don't bite, do they?'

'No, they don't,' said her mate. 'Anyway, it's not a butterfly. It's a moth.'

Louise jerked her head away suddenly, like somebody had presented her with a teaspoon of shite. The moth fluttered away. She watched it, repulsed, and rubbed her nose with her hand.

It was every bit as beautiful as the butterfly she thought it was, but not to her. Not any more. Because she was told it was a moth. And as it fluttered back towards her, she ducked and dived like a boxer, trying to smack the thing out of existence. Her mate had to grab her arm and pull her away. They left the park, with Louise still wiping her nose, her day ruined.

What the fuck is her problem, man?

STREET LIGHTS

He'd looked it all up, how to do it. How to fuck with the traffic lights. From one place you could control the traffic lights for the whole city, turn them all off, turn them all red, amber, green. You could make them all flash like a disco if you wanted. But he didn't.

If he was a terrorist, he would have turned them all green. Drivers would speed through green light after green light, thinking it was their lucky day, until they turned their head to see another lucky driver heading in from the side. But he wasn't a terrorist.

He could have turned them all red. If he was some kind of anti-capitalist activist, he would have jumped at the chance. Right in the middle of rush hour, he could have stopped the rat race right in its tracks and dealt a crushing blow to the Man. But not him. Call him a bore or a fascist, but that wasn't for him.

He turned them all amber.

The world was moving too fast. He didn't want to

put on the red lights, he didn't want to cause a major disruption, he wasn't against people earning a bit of money, he didn't want anybody to lose their job. He just wanted everybody to slow down a bit, that's all. They would slow down, and then stop, for a while. They'd stop long enough to look over to the other drivers in the other motors, to decide on what to do. Who's to go first? Me? You? Their eyes would meet, they'd sit in their cars communicating with hand gestures, with shrugs, with smiles. People would step out their motors and talk. That's all he wanted. He just wanted people to talk, to each other. To slow down and talk. They'd talk about what's going on, they'd maybe laugh, and realise that they weren't in such a hurry after all.

That was the plan.

What happened was in many ways worse than if he had just set all the lights to green. People got confused, they felt like idiots, they got defensive and angry. They got out their motors, not to chat and laugh, but to argue. People swore in front of other people's children, people were told to watch their fucking language, people were told they could say whatever the fuck they wanted and you better get that fucking look off your face, mate, I'm warning you. People got battered, some got killed. Two guys started fighting with each other over a broken tail light, until some other guy tried to break it up, at which point the two guys put their differences aside to murder the do-gooder with a car jack – before all three of them were run over by a 70mph amber-gambler hoping to beat the camera, who himself died after being decapitated by his seatbelt.

So the plan didn't work out.

But at least it got them talking.

THE TEACUP

Billy was about sixty. He was walking through some spare ground, walking back home from feeding the birds. And it was there he saw the teacup.

It was a dainty wee thing, a white cup with flowers painted on it and a gold rim at the top, lying there in the grass next to some broken bottles and a used johnny bag. It looked old-fashioned, like something you'd see on the *Antiques Roadshow*. It looked like it might be worth something. He knew it wouldn't be, otherwise it wouldn't be lying here, but it was worth something to him anyway; it looked nice, simple as that, and he'd like to have it. It was probably cracked, though, knowing his luck, so he picked it up and had a look, bracing himself for disappointment. But there were no cracks to be found. No cracks, no scratches, not even a speck of dirt. After lying there in that tip, not one speck of dirt. That was strange. But good. He put it in his pocket and carried on walking home, a wee bit chirpier than before.

When he got there, he took the cup out his pocket
and went into the kitchen to see if he had any tea bags.
He quite fancied the idea of sipping tea out of his new
teacup. He was a whisky man, usually. Well, he used to
be a whisky man, to be more accurate. He knocked the
whole thing on the head six months ago. That's partly
why he was off feeding the birds. The folk at AA told
him it would be good for him, to get out the house, get
out the pub, just go for walks and breathe in the fresh
air. He felt a bit daft feeding birds to begin with, a man
like him, and he took some slagging for it. Eventually,
though, he just thought the slagging was interesting. It
was interesting to observe. They were fine with him
queuing outside the pub at eight in the morning, they
were all right with him having to get carried home at
the end of the night. That was Billy for you. What a
legend. But going for a walk in the park to feed the
birds? What the fuck was he playing at? What a joke.

He looked in the cupboard and picked up the box
of tea bags. He was looking forward to this. He
wondered how his old mates would feel if they saw
him with his teacup, sipping tea in his living room,
watching the *Antiques Roadshow*, his legs crossed, his
pinky out, haha. But that would have to wait, because
when he looked in the box, it was empty. No fucking
tea bags, oh come on, man. There were the remnants
of a burst tea bag along the edges of the cupboard
shelf. If he was desperate enough, he could slide it all
into the teacup, but the tea leaves would also come

with year-old crumbs and hair and bits of dead flies, and he wasn't that desperate.

'Och, I really fancied a cuppa,' he mumbled.

And then something happened.

First, he smelled it. Then he looked down and saw it. He rubbed his eyes, looked away, then looked back. But there it was, and as real as you like. The teacup had somehow been topped up with tea. Piping-hot tea.

He reached for a kitchen knife, because there was only one conclusion you could come to here: somebody had broken in. He searched the kitchen, and found nobody. He searched around the house, opening each door slowly before bursting into the room, stabbing at nothing. After five minutes of checking and double-checking, he came back to the teacup and stared. He didn't know who was behind all this, but he'd be fucked if he was drinking it. It was poisoned. Maybe. Or maybe after drinking it he'd conk out and wake up somewhere he didn't want to be.

He poured the tea into the sink, put the cup back down on the kitchen worktop, and stared at it some more. Somebody must have sneaked in right under his fucking nose and filled the cup with tea, from a flask, then sneaked out. Or maybe he filled it himself, then blacked out. Or maybe . . .

Could it be?

Try it again. Go.

He had another look around, in case this was some kind of wind-up. He looked around for people, he looked for hidden cameras and microphones. He found nothing.

He closed the blinds in case they were filming from outside. He even pointed out to whoever was listening, if anybody was listening, that he knew that this was just a wind-up but he was going to go along with it. He looked back at the cup.

'I fancy a cuppa,' he said to the cup. And he discovered that this was no wind-up. He had seen some things in his time, including things that weren't really there, but he'd never seen anything like this. The teacup began to fill up with tea. Some doubt still remained: perhaps there was a pipe underneath the cup feeding the tea into it, perhaps they had cut a wee hole in the worktop underneath in the exact position where he put the cup down, with some kind of silent saw, which also sawed through the bottom of the cup, and then they put a wee tube through the cup and pumped the tea in. Somehow. He knew the chances of pulling off a stunt like that were slim, but they weren't as slim as the alternative explanation. He picked up the cup, not sure what he'd prefer to see.

There was no tube. The tea continued to fill to the top of the cup, right there in his hand, right before his eyes. That was it decided then.

It was a magic teacup.

He brought the cup to his mouth, and sipped. He didn't know what to expect. Maybe tea from a magic teacup was, in itself, magic. Maybe it would make him float. Maybe it would taste, I don't know, twinkly. But as it turned out, it was better than that. It was quite simply the perfect cup of tea.

When he was finished, he put the cup down on the worktop, stared at it for a while, and had a thought. What else could the teacup make?

'I quite fancy a cup of that Earl Grey or whatever it's called.'

The magic teacup filled up with a cup of Earl Grey, as requested. He had a few gulps. It was nice, but it wasn't his thing. He emptied it into the sink and thought of something else.

'I'd like a herbal tea,' he said, not quite sure what a herbal tea was. But he got one all the same. He had a sip then put it in the sink. 'Can you give me a coffee?' A coffee was served. 'Hot chocolate!' A delicious hot chocolate. This was brilliant!

'Gie's a triple whisky!'

Oh dear.

He didn't mean it. It was just habit. Whenever he felt all jovial and in high spirits, he'd just bark it out – in the old days, that was. He was just about to cancel his order, but the teacup got in there first. Here you are, sir, a triple whisky in a teacup. Enjoy.

He had no intention of drinking it, but he didn't pour it out right away. He just stared. It looked like whisky, that's for sure. He wasn't used to seeing it within a white teacup, mind you, but that was whisky all right. He brought it up to his face – not to drink it, Jesus, not to drink it – just to smell it. And, aye, it smelled like whisky. A very nice whisky.

He should have put it down. But he didn't.

Would it taste like whisky? The teacup could make the perfect cup of tea, but could it make the perfect cup of whisky? He wasn't sure if he'd ever had a perfect whisky; he'd certainly never had a magic whisky. He wondered what it would taste like. Just one sip. Just one. It doesn't really count, does it? A sip of whisky that came from a magic teacup? He didn't think that was against the rules. They didn't mention that in AA. Well, of course they didn't, but, you know. It doesn't really count, does it?

He had a sip. Just a sip.

Twenty cups later, he was blitzed, and fast asleep on the kitchen floor. As for the cup, it was smashed. He bumped the thing over when he went to the toilet, smashed it to pieces on the kitchen tiles. And that was that. The end.

No, I mean it. That's it. The end.

Alky fucking bastard.

I mean, for the love of fuck. No offence to those who have been affected by alcoholism, I've been affected myself. At the time of writing this I've been off the demon drink for ten years, so no offence intended. But this story was going somewhere. He could have filled the teacup with diamonds or gold or a cure for fucking cancer, but no. He didn't even do that thing he wanted to do with the pinky and the crossed legs in the living room in front of the *Antiques Roadshow*, remember that? He said he was looking forward to it. Maybe you were as well. I know I was. But we can forget about that now.

Alky bastard.

Stupid, selfish, alky bastard.

A VALUED MEMBER OF THE TEAM

Gerry was sitting at his desk at work with nothing to do. That would be fine, normally; most people would love something like that. You could check your Twitter, Facebook, check the news to see if anything had happened. Not many people would complain about being in that position. But Gerry had been doing nothing since he started at the company. That was almost three years now.

You might be thinking that I don't really mean he was doing nothing, that I mean he was doing little. No, I mean he was doing nothing. When he started, he assumed that somebody would come along at some point and tell him what work he should do, but it hadn't happened, nobody had spoken to him. It wasn't that he was being given the silent treatment, it wasn't that the rest of the office couldn't stand him, far from it. He was very popular in the company, perhaps the most popular employee in the whole floor of over a hundred employees. That's if you could call him an employee. Because, seriously, he did fuck all.

Three years doing fuck all. Maybe it was time to say
something. He didn't want to be rude, but maybe it was
time. His boss walked past. Now was the time.

'Can I speak to you, Mags?' he said.

'Sure, Gerry! How are you today?' said Mags.

Gerry told her that he'd been doing nothing since he
arrived at the company three years ago. She laughed it
off, saying he should count himself lucky, she wished she
had nothing to do. She was so busy!

No, he'd really like something to do, he told her. Once
he started being a bit adamant about it, his confidence
grew, and Mags could tell that it was time to speak to
him. Time to speak to him about the whole thing. Some
heads were turning towards the conversation. It looked
like it was time.

'Gerry,' she said. 'You're paid good money, I don't see
what the problem is.'

'But what for?' asked Gerry. 'What do I actually do?
I don't do anything.'

Some people around chipped in with support for Gerry,
telling him he did plenty and was a valued member of
the team. Gerry turned to see that pretty much the whole
office had stopped working to see this conversation, like
it was a long time coming. Gerry could see people craning
their heads for a look. Some came over and stroked his
head.

'Gerry,' said Mags. 'You know how some offices have,
like, maybe a cat or a dog?'

'Aye.'

'You know, a dog or cat that belongs to somebody in the office and they bring it in and, you know, it's supposed to reduce stress in the workplace and it's good for productivity and so on?'

'Aye,' said Gerry. 'But what's this got to do with me?'

'Well,' said Mags, as she shifted her weight from one foot to the other and tried to find the right words. Gerry looked around the office at all the sympathetic smiles directed towards him.

'Nobody in the office has a dog or cat,' Mags continued. 'And it didn't seem right to buy a pet just for the office, one that belonged to the company. What if we went bust? We'd have to throw the thing in the river. So we thought, well . . .'

Gerry raised his palm and closed his eyes: he didn't want to hear another word. Mags got the message, and stopped talking. This was strange and upsetting. Gerry didn't know what to do. He opened his mouth to speak . . .

Somebody kicked a ball; Gerry chased after it. He got it!

He was going to say something. Or was he? He couldn't remember.

Anyway, the ball. He got it!

THE CHIMNEY

'The fucking state of these skirting boards,' said Kenny. 'I'm going to phone the solicitor.'

'Don't be fucking stupid – phone them for what?' asked Julie.

'Well, they didn't tell us the skirting boards were wonky when we bought the flat. We could get money from the last lot to fix it.'

'Don't be fucking stupid,' said Julie again.

'Well, what about that rattling sound when you flush the toilet?' said Kenny. 'They didn't tell us about that.'

'Kenny, it's an old building. We knew that.' Julie had a thought. 'Here, I've got an idea: how d'you fancy trying out the fireplace?'

She and Kenny had moved into the flat a few weeks ago: an old tenement, loads of character. It had done nothing but piss Kenny off, but Julie loved all its wee quirks. She especially loved that fireplace – it was almost half the reason why she had bought the place. Julie had only lived in new builds, so what a novelty it would be to go and get coal, actual real coal, stick it in the fireplace, an actual real fireplace, and get a fire on the go. Not some fake fire, not that cheesy projection thing you got inside electric fires, but an actual real fire. Kenny agreed, but didn't want to seem too enthusiastic. If he couldn't find coal in any of the cupboards, forget it. No way he was going to the shops and carrying a bag of coal up three flights of stairs like something out a fucking Charles Dickens novel. So he played it cool, he didn't want to get her hopes up, he didn't want anybody making assumptions.

He had a look in the cupboard next to the living room, which was full of the previous owner's unwanted stuff: a broken clothes horse; a child's toy garage without the cars; one of those poles you can extend inside the top of a door frame to do pull-ups. Stuff like that. Rubbish like that. Kenny was about to moan for the millionth time about that last lot, all the wee things they didn't tell him about, and all the wee things they said they were going to do which they didn't, like when they said they would take all their shite with them. He was fucking itching to phone those solicitors, but he forgot all about it when he spotted the bag of coal. All was forgiven. For now.

He dragged the bag over to the fireplace. It was heavy as fuck. Julie told him to not scratch the floor. Kenny reminded her that they were getting a carpet put down, so it didn't matter. She reminded Kenny that they hadn't agreed on that, they were just thinking about it. Kenny asked her if she wanted this fire or not; she said yes. But he wasn't to scratch the floor.

Kenny opened the bag and started putting some coal in the fireplace, before remembering that you had to put wee bits of wood down first. Kindling, it was called. He had another look in the cupboard to see if that last lot had left some kindling next to where the bag of coal was, and thank fuck, they had. He decided, right, he'd just forget about phoning the solicitors. That last lot had saved him a lot of hassle, twice in two minutes. He'd forget all about it, that was that decided.

So eventually, after a few false starts, they got a fire going. Then Julie switched off the light.

'Romantic, isn't it?' she said.

'Aye,' said Kenny, not totally agreeing. 'Bit smoky, though, d'you not think?'

'I love that smell,' said Julie, taking a big sniff. 'Kind of makes you feel like—'

'No, it's too smoky,' said Kenny. 'You're meant to smell it a bit, but not this much. Switch the light on.'

'No, keep the light off,' said Julie. 'A big bright fucking lightbulb over our head? How cosy.'

'Seriously, Julie,' he said. 'Switch it fucking on, eh? It's too fucking smoky.'

'No.'

Kenny tutted, then stood up and walked over to the door. He hit the light switch, and his suspicions were confirmed. Smoke everywhere, man. Smoke billowing everywhere.

'Fuck!' shouted Julie, looking at the dark smoke filling up the freshly furnished room. 'Open the windows, quick!' They ran to the windows and opened them up, letting the smoke out and the winter air in. It was fucking baltic. Kenny looked at the smoke still coming from the fire. He saw the tongs hanging from the wee fireplace tool stand and toyed with the idea of using them to lob the coal out the window. He visualised what burning coal would do to somebody's head if it was dropped from three floors up, and decided against it.

'Get water!' shouted Julie. Good idea. Off he ran and back he came with water in a pint glass, spilling most of it on the floor in the process. He poured it over the coal. Steam and water everywhere. Steam, and water as black as soot, everywhere. What a fucking shambles. The fire was out, but what a shambles.

When the smoke had cleared, they shut the windows and sat back down on the couch, not saying anything for a bit. Maybe not wanting to, because they weren't sure who was to blame. Eventually Julie made the first move, with a fairly neutral, 'So what happened?'

'I don't know,' shrugged Kenny, before standing up and heading over to the fireplace, slipping on the spilt water and nearly falling on his arse. Kenny looked to Julie to see if that brought some comic relief, but no. He looked back to the fireplace. 'I think the chimney's blocked,' he said, crouching down and inspecting it to see if he was right. He couldn't see, it was dark up there. He got out his phone, stuck on the torch and had another look.

He couldn't believe his eyes.

He looked around at Julie slowly. She could tell something was seriously up. 'Kenny, what is it?' she said, worried. 'Tell me.'

'It's . . .' Kenny had trouble finishing what he was about to say. He put his hand up the chimney and held on to what he saw, partly to make sure he wasn't imagining it, and partly because he was about to pull it down to prove to Julie that he hadn't lost his mind.

'Julie,' said Kenny, before giving the thing a yank. 'It's Santa.'

Before Julie had the chance to say 'Fucking shut up', down came Kenny's proof from the chimney, crashing into the fireplace and knocking the tongs and other tools flying. It was the corpse of Father Christmas, followed by a couple of dead pigeons.

Kenny looked down at the body in its tattered, chimney-stained clothes. It looked like a cross between the Santa that he knew and loved and a zombie.

Julie inhaled to scream, but stopped when the elves appeared. Three of them, out of nowhere. Pop, pop, pop! She inhaled again and fell back on the couch. She couldn't remember if her next breath should be in or out. She was stumped.

The elves explained that they'd been looking for Santa everywhere since last Christmas, and thanked Kenny for finding him. Now, they announced with pleasure, it would be Kenny's turn to be Santa.

'What?' said Kenny to the elves.

Elves?

What the fuck?

The elves explained that that's how it worked. Oh, it wasn't the first time Santa had died, it happened every few years, whether it was getting stuck down a chimney and dying of suffocation, or falling 20,000 feet from the sleigh, steaming drunk. The elves would just find a replacement, no big deal. And Kenny would be that replacement, if he'd like to just come along nicely.

'No fucking way,' said Kenny, pushing one of the elves. Kenny noticed that pushing the elf only pushed himself away. It was like pushing a brick wall. Although the elf was only half the height of Kenny, the wee prick was solid.

'Very well,' said the elf, turning to Julie. 'Then it will be you. Come.'

The elves walked towards her, and she started booting at them. 'Fuck off. Get yourselves to fuck, fuck off!'

'No,' shouted Kenny. 'Take me! Take me!'

'First answer counts, mate,' said one of the elves, a wee jobsworthy type. Kenny tried pulling one of the elves back, but he may as well have been pulling at a lamp-post and expecting it to budge. The elf swung his arm, throwing Kenny through the air as effortlessly as a bull goring a seven-stone junkie.

'Take me,' groaned Kenny as he fell against the wall. But it was too late. As the elves put their hands on Julie, she started to change. She began ageing, at a rate of five years a second. Her face began growing that familiar white beard. And she got fat as fuck.

She inhaled one last time, and Kenny braced himself for an ear-piercing scream. He didn't brace himself for this, though . . .

'Ho ho ho!' she boomed, with the voice of an over-weight man in his sixties. Kenny would never forget the look of surprise on her face when she heard that come out. And then pop! She and her elves were gone.

Kenny lay in the corner of the living room, in the silence, wondering if what had just happened really did just happen.

But it did. He didn't know how, but it did.

Kenny shook his head.

He was going to phone the solicitors after all.

Tomorrow morning, first fucking thing.

THE BOWLING CLUB

Stuart got handed a flyer. Normally if he got handed a flyer, it would be from some young guy or lassie to promote a club or a special offer in a shop nearby. But this flyer was from an old guy, for a bowling club. Haha. He couldn't help laughing.

He looked at the old guy, there with his navy-blue blazer and his thinning ginger hair, not too happy about being laughed at. Probably sick to death of these young ones having no manners. 'Where is it?' asked Stuart, feeling that he owed the old guy a bit of small talk after hurting his feelings. The old guy wasn't up for talking; he just pointed to a gate in the hedge behind him, still in a mood. It would take a lot more than small talk to make it up to the poor old fellow. Stuart had a spare few minutes, so he thought, Fuck it, and through the gate he walked.

He walked down the path and around the building, following the sound of bowls gently hitting off other bowls and the sound of old folk chatting. He didn't hear many young people, and wondered if maybe they were indoors, inside the building. He wondered why anybody his age would want to come to a place like this anyway. Maybe the booze was cheap.

Eventually he reached the bowling green, and saw the people there bowling. At a glance he could see that all these people were old, not a young face amongst them. There were men and women, wearing all that lawn bowls attire, the white jumpers and trousers and skirts, all of them old, some old as fuck. Over to the left of the green he could see a group of old dears having a game, three women with ginger hair, having a natter. Over at the other side were a group of old but not old-old men, also with ginger hair, taking things very seriously.

Hell of a lot of ginger folk in here.

And there in the middle were two very, very old men playing a one-on-one match, maybe a grudge match that had lasted for decades. They were wearing hats. A gust of wind blew off one of their hats, revealing a head of ginger hair.

Ginger. Again?

The ginger guy who had lost his hat was about to chase after it, but the other guy offered to give him his. He took off his hat, revealing his hair to also be ginger.

This was all getting strange. And it didn't seem quite right.

Stuart thought he'd seen enough, hopefully enough to make that old guy out there on the street a bit cheerier.

Mind you, the old guy wasn't his top reason for leaving. He'd just really like to leave now. He turned to walk out, and in doing so, he got a glance inside the bowling club through the windows that faced the lawn. It was busy, full of lots of older folk whiling away their time. No young people. None.

And all of them were ginger.

Stuart made a run for it.

He sprinted down the path and back around the building, not looking behind to see if they were on his heels. He shot out the gate in the hedge and onto the street, with the intention of running for another few minutes for safe measure. But that was soon brought to a halt.

'Away so soon?' asked the old guy with the flyers, standing in Stuart's way.

'What the fuck's going on?' asked Stuart. He could easily have just run away from all this, but he needed to find out. 'They're ginger. They're all ginger!'

'Yes,' said the old guy. 'They are. But so are you!'

Stuart felt his head tingle. He turned to one of the parked motors at his side and looked at his reflection in the window. And sure enough, his hair was changing colour, from jet black to carrot orange. He looked to the old guy to ask what the bloody hell was going on here, and saw that the old guy's ginger hair was turning black.

'And here,' said the old guy, 'here you shall remain. Like I have for many, many years. At this gate, with these flyers, a ginger, until you can find someone to replace you. This is where I bid you farewell.'

The old guy was about to hand over the flyers, but Stuart just said, 'Fuck that,' and carried on running. Stuart's hair started turning back to black, as the old guy's hair turned back to ginger.

The old guy watched Stuart run away. No point in chasing after him – nothing he could do. You know, he'd had just about enough of this. The old guy really was sick to death of these young ones. The way they'd run off like that. No manners. Out of control. No respect for the rules, no respect for their elders. And there really is nothing you can do. You can't give them a clout round the ear, you can't grab their arm, you can't even lay a finger on them or else they'll get you done for assault.

That's why this country's gone to pot.

THE GLOBE

He was walking through a bookshop, just having a look.
Just killing some time during his lunch break until he
had to head back to work, back to his shite job. He liked
coming in here. It was one of those big bookshops with
four floors and a lift and a coffee shop inside; it was a
nice wee escape. He'd never actually buy anything,
though, or be one of those people who sat on the floor
with a book in their hands, all wrapped up in a world
of their own. It was just a nice place to wander around,
occasionally picking up something that had an interesting
cover, looking at the description on the back, then
returning it to the shelf. It kind of reminded him of
going to the video shop when he was a boy, surrounded
by all these covers, scary ones, romantic ones, funny
ones, all designed to attract your eye and draw you in
and get you wondering. Aye, it was a nice wee escape,
this, a nice wee getaway.

He looked at the time and sighed: time to head back

before he got another talking-to for being late. He walked down the stairs to the ground floor and off towards the door, stopping for a second or two to look at the stuff near the tills: notepads and pens, board games, pocket-sized books of inspirational quotes, stuff like that, the bookshop equivalent of the chocolate temptations they have at supermarket checkouts. They had a wee globe, an inflatable one about the size of a football, sitting on top of a stack of atlases. He picked it up and had a look at it, not that he was going to buy it, but you do that sometimes when you see a globe, you have a wee look. You maybe tell yourself you're going to go to one of the countries one day, but will you fuck. He looked at the first country he saw, Japan, and gave it a tap with his finger. One day, he thought. One day. He didn't know why, it wasn't one of his lifelong ambitions to go to Japan or anything, but it would be good to get away, to Japan or anywhere else. He put down the globe and off he went, back to finish his shite day at his shite job.

When he got home that night, he headed to the kitchen to make himself some dinner, stepping into the living room briefly to turn on the telly before walking out – he liked a bit of noise on. In the kitchen, he got a pot out the cupboard, stuck it on the worktop and held a handful of spaghetti over it, getting ready to break it in two.

He froze.

He just heard something from the news next door. Something about . . . he couldn't remember now. Something had made him stop, he didn't know what. He got ready to break the spaghetti once more, then he heard it again. Something the reporter said. He walked through to the living room to make sure he wasn't hearing things. Maybe he was just imagining it. But no.

There had been an earthquake in Japan.

And it wasn't just one of those wee ones where they show you CCTV footage of filing cabinets wobbling about in an office. It wasn't something you'd see in some compilation programme of funny home videos where the studio audience would laugh at people falling about daft. It was the kind of thing where the newsreader warns you that some viewers may find the following scenes disturbing.

That's unbelievable. He was only just thinking about Japan today, and then this happens. How often does he think about Japan? Not that often. But today, for no reason, he walked over to that globe, picked it up and looked at Japan. He even gave it a wee tap with his finger. And then this happens. That's like some kind of premonition, surely.

Wait. Wait a minute.

He gave Japan a wee tap with his finger. And then this. An earthquake!

No, don't be silly. Don't be silly, now. He switched off the news and went back to the kitchen to finish making his dinner, and didn't give it another thought. Some coincidence, though, eh?

A couple of weeks later, back he was in the bookshop. No, nothing to do with the globe – he'd got himself caught out in the rain during his lunch break, and bolted indoors before he got soaked top to bottom. And, as usual, he wandered around between the floors, looking at book covers and descriptions, at biographies of people he'd never heard of, and at classics that he'd always heard of but never read. He looked at the time; it was time to head back. He looked out the window; it was still pouring. Fuck off. So he walked down the stairs to the ground floor, and had one last look at the stuff around the tills. Things had changed a bit since the last time he was in, a few things had come and gone, but one thing remained: the globe.

He picked it up, gently. His heart raced slightly, as he wondered what he'd do if he saw that Japan was gone. But that, again, was just fucking silly. Japan itself, the actual country, wasn't gone, the earthquake didn't sink Japan into the sea like Atlantis, and even if Japan was missing from an inflatable globe, it would be a printing error: a highly coincidental printing error, but a printing error nonetheless. He turned the globe slowly towards Japan, and saw that Japan was still intact. He was relieved.

He looked out the door to the rain he'd be running out into, and looked back at the globe. He quite fancied getting away from all this, to somewhere warm. He looked at Spain, to Brazil, before finally resting his eyes on India. Now there's an interesting place, so they say. He almost gave it a tap with his finger, then thought twice. C'mon, now, don't be silly. Don't be fucking silly.

You can't tap a country on a blow-up globe and cause a tragedy, it's unheard of. So he touched it. He didn't want to, but he felt he had to, just to put this silliness behind him. One touch. Not a tap-tap-tap, just a touch. Then he put down the globe, walked to the door and sprinted into the pissing rain.

When he got home that night, he walked straight to the living room, his jacket still on, turned on the telly and flipped to the news. Nothing. He got out his phone to check out the news online, in case he missed the headline on the telly. Nothing. Nothing about India anyway. What was he expecting? He smiled and went to the kitchen and made himself some dinner. Business as usual.

Until five weeks later.

He was having dinner. Watching the news. And he saw something that stopped him mid munch. There had been a flood. In India! Well, it was Sri Lanka, to be exact, but that was close enough. He had touched that fucking globe just after coming in from the rain. It was five weeks ago, but he remembered it clearly: it was raining, and he touched India (pretty much) with what was probably a wet finger, and now they've got a flood. Are you going to call that a coincidence? No, that was that as far as he was concerned. That was fucking that. What time was it, what time did that bookshop shut?

An hour later he returned from the bookshop with the globe in a bag. The display model. They wouldn't let him have it, to begin with, because it would mean one of the staff would have to replace it by removing a new one from its box and blowing it up. But he insisted, offering to blow it up for them; he just wanted that display one. He needed it. So they gave him it. They told him he didn't have to blow up a new one, though, the shop was shutting and they just wanted to go home. So now it was his.

He looked at it as it sat on the kitchen worktop. He looked at it without moving an inch. Fear and awe, that's what he was feeling. What was this thing? Who made it, and how could it hold so much power? He turned his head to hear a woman outside in the street, telling her son to hurry up and stop eating from the bags, it'll ruin his dinner. The normality gave him a shake, and when he looked back to the kitchen worktop, all he saw was an inflatable globe. Probably cost no more than twenty pence to make. He burst out laughing. Dear fucking God, man, what the fuck? Had he lost it? What the fuck had he done? Haha. A globe with magical powers, is that really what he thought? He felt like taking a knife to it to prove a point, but he quite liked the thing. He put it in the cupboard and gave his mates a phone. Fuck me, if there was a guy that needed to get out the house, it was him. It'd been too long.

It lasted three minutes. One of his mates in the pub said something about global warming. He remembered the globe was in the cupboard next to the tumble dryer. The dryer wasn't on, no, but the significance was there. He stood up and ran out without saying a word. When he got home, he took the globe out the cupboard – very, very fucking gently – and placed it next to the draught at his bedroom window.

Six weeks later there was a hurricane somewhere. How's about that then?

He moved the globe back to the kitchen, this time just keeping it on the worktop. All was well, until he saw a fly land somewhere in Africa.

Two months later there was something on the telly about malaria. Fancy that.

He moved it to the living room and placed it on the couch, where it wasn't too hot, it wasn't too cold, where he could pull up a seat and sit nearby and keep his eyes on it and make sure no flies or spiders or anything else could get near it without him seeing it first. He could sit there all day, all night, with the news on by his side to keep him updated on world affairs. All week long.

The lads texted to try and get him out, they were concerned, but he was busy. His work got in touch to ask him where he was, and then they got in touch to let him go, but he was busy. The bank and the council and folk like that sent him letters with red ink and capital letters to tell him that he had to do this and that urgently or else. But sorry, he was busy.

A year later there was a conference, one of these big conferences where the world's leaders get together to discuss how to save the planet. As they stood outside for their group photo, protesters waved banners and shouted things to say that the leaders weren't doing enough.

Peaceful protesters, of course, staying well behind the barrier. All except one.

He leapt over the barrier and made a run for the leaders. He looked wild. You could barely see his face for hair. It was difficult to tell where the hair on his head stopped and the beard began. Completely fucking wild. And completely naked.

Because he was naked, the marksmen decided he wasn't a threat, and let the police on the ground take care of it. Until they saw the bomb. At least, it looked like a bomb. Not the type of bomb you strap to yourself to blow you and everybody else up, but like a cartoon bomb. A big round thing you carry in your hands. It was the size of a football and . . . they didn't know, but you can't hesitate with that kind of thing, not for a moment.

The wild man was babbling as he raced towards the leaders, something about how he'd destroy the planet if they didn't come together to find a solution. Maybe. They couldn't be sure, he was too far away, and he didn't get much closer. One bullet tore through his shoulder and knocked him to the ground. The next bullet punctured the bomb, proving it to be not a bomb but an inflatable something or other. He just seemed like a relatively harmless fruitcake. But the marksmen put another half a dozen bullets into his head anyway, just to be on the safe side.

And that was the end of that.

Insane, you might think. An insane, naked loony lying next to a burst, inflatable globe. Is that what you think? Well, perhaps you're right. But consider this.

Not long after the globe exploded, so did our planet. No, not right away, not by our minuscule measure of time. I'm talking a billion, billion, billion years later. But it exploded nevertheless. And that kind of time, in the scale of the infinite universe, well, that's practically a moment.

Now, I don't know about you. But that seems like a mighty strange coincidence to me.

ONE MAN HUNT

Daniel wanted to play. He was sad because he wanted to play but nobody would play with him. No, he wasn't a six-year-old boy, he was a forty-one-year-old man. But nevertheless, he wanted to play. He'd tried most of the grown-up ways to play. Shagging, drugs, going to things. Football, gambling, *Farm Ville*. You name it. They were all good for a while, then they weren't. Same old, same old. It was like there was nothing left. Nothing at all. Except, there was one thing.

D'you know what he fancied? D'you know what he fancied playing? This'll sound daft. He knew it sounded daft, but the more tired he grew of all these things that were supposed to entertain him, the less daft it felt. It almost felt like the only other option. D'you know what he fancied? He fancied a game of one man hunt.

It was a game they'd play when he was a boy; he hadn't played it for fucking ages. He loved it. It was a bit like hide and seek, in that everybody would run and

hide and one person would count to a hundred then go
and try and find them. The difference was that instead
of just spotting the person, you had to grab them and
shout, 'Two, four, six, eight, ten, caught, one man hunt!'
Then that newly grabbed person would join in the
hunting, then the next, then the next. You'd all be
climbing over walls, hiding under motors, jumping
through hedges, pissing the neighbours off to fuck. And
the more people that were caught, the more mental it
would get, because the people who were the best at
getting away were the people that were into taking the
most risks, like climbing drainpipes and running onto
roofs and hanging off things by the tips of their fingers.
It was insane. It was deadly. It was fucking magic.

But then everybody grew up. They lost interest. There
was a time when everybody was up for it, everybody
you knew was up for a game, then, one by one, they'd
stop. They'd just stop, never to play again. And if you
asked, they'd laugh at you, like you were a silly wee boy,
like you'd asked them if they wanted to play with your
My Little Pony. Usually it was an overnight thing: they
were into a game yesterday, but today, no, as if a part
of their childhood had died in its sleep. But for some, it
would happen while the game was playing, it would
happen mid-game. Everybody would hide, waiting for
the guy to come hunting, but the guy wouldn't come. At
some point during counting, it would occur to the guy
that this wasn't his thing any more and he'd just head
home. He'd just head up the road without telling anybody.

But Daniel never lost interest. He never let it go. He kept it to himself, of course, he didn't want to look like a freak. But he always wondered if anybody else felt like him. He wondered if anybody else felt like him now. So he sent out a wee tweet. He just chucked the thought out there: he tweeted, 'Anybody up for a game of one man hunt?' He only had around forty followers, who were mates, mates of mates, and some strangers that had started following him after a few of his funnier tweets got retweeted. He didn't expect much of a reply, which was just as well. Most people said nothing. A few just said, 'No.' One asked if the game was iOS only, because they looked it up on Android and couldn't find it.

Pish.

He wasn't being completely serious when he suggested the idea, but it was a pish response anyway. He read one more tweet. One of his followers said he'd be up for it, and suggested that Daniel could start a Facebook group to get everybody together. Daniel laughed at how pathetic that sounded, and that surprised him. It appalled him, in fact. He felt like one of the boys that would laugh at him for asking if they fancied a game, the ones that had gone off it, the ones that were in a hurry to grow up. And he did not want to be one of them. No, he'd do this. He'd do it for that wee boy inside him that wondered why the fun had stopped, the wee boy that got dragged into gambling, drugs and *FarmVille* when all he ever wanted was a game of one man hunt.

So he started a group, and called it 'Who's Up For a

Game of One Man Hunt?' He put in the time, date and location of when and where it would be, along with a description of why he wanted to do it. It took him ages to type that description, far longer than he thought, typing and deleting in the middle of the night, getting more and more emotional the later it got. What he thought would just be a fun wee paragraph had turned into a thousand-word essay on his own personal journey and the deep-and-meaningful purpose of finding like-minded individuals for this childhood game, this physical, non-digital, human game. It sounded wanky as fuck, he knew it, but he posted it anyway, and then went to sleep.

When he woke up the next day, the group had already attracted a few dozen members, with all of them saying they'd be there. By the end of the day, after word spread of this wacky but cool wee idea, the numbers had grown to a few hundred. A few hundred people saying they'd be up for a game of one man hunt. Well, he'd always wondered if anybody else felt like him, and now he knew. He was buzzing.

When the day came, Daniel cycled to the spare ground where he'd suggested they meet. He imagined that nobody would have turned up, not really. People do things like that, they click buttons saying they'll be attending something or other, but all they mean is they think it's a nice idea, that's all. But he was wrong. A crowd of around fifty people turned to welcome him with a cheer. Aye, it was a lot less than the people who said they'd be there, but it was still a fair size, and it would without a doubt be the biggest game of one man hunt he had ever played.

After the cheer, he didn't quite know what to say; he'd never done anything like this before. There was a moment when it all went quiet as people waited for him to speak, then a few people started speaking at once. One guy asked if they all fancied heading to a pub after the game; he was wearing a leather jacket, even though it was roasting, and it looked like he had come by himself. There was a fat guy in his late forties who seemed to have not accepted his hair loss, brushing the remains of it forward over his forehead whenever the wind blew it back; he told Daniel that it was good to get out the house and he hoped to make some good friends that day. There was a teenage guy who kept looking away whenever Daniel made eye contact with him.

Daniel told them all that he thought it would be a good idea to just get the game under way. Before he arrived, he'd fantasised about shouting, 'It's time to start running!' like the presenter from *The Running Man*, but for whatever reason, he didn't. He started to count, and watched them as they made a run for it. One guy was wearing a washed-out Prince tour T-shirt from 1988. Another guy in the distance was climbing into a metal barrel, not seeming to mind that he was being covered in oil, the way a normal person would mind. And another guy was climbing a drainpipe, just like boys did when Daniel was young. Except he wasn't young, and it didn't look right, like when Michael Jackson climbed that tree.

When everybody was out of sight, Daniel stopped counting. He stopped counting halfway in.

He remembered the guy in the leather jacket suggesting they go to the pub. And the balding guy hoping to make some good friends that day. And that teenage guy that had problems with making eye contact.

And then Daniel headed up the road.

He headed up the road without telling anybody.

THE GAMBLER

The pub was empty. He got a pint at the bar and walked over to the fruit machine. He stuck a few quid in, but he knew it was pointless. It never ended well, this. It never ended with a jackpot and a round of drinks for the house. It ended with nothing. It always did.

In less than a minute, three quid was gone. Just like that.

He put his hand in his pocket and dug out some change. He had maybe a fiver. A couple of pound coins, some fifties, some other change. He was going to shove the two pound coins in one after the other, but thought he'd just put one in now and see how it went.

He got nothing.

He stuck in the other pound, and got nothing.

He put his hand in his pocket to get out the other change, and banged in three fifties. Nothing.

He put his hand in his pocket and shoved in the rest of the change, he didn't know how much. He just shoved the lot in.

Nothing.

Mind you, on the last shot there, the wee numbers on the reels added up to three. He needed four exactly to get onto the feature thing. One of the numbers on the reels was one, so if he put in more money and got a hold, he could hold the number one, spin the rest, and hopefully no other numbers would come in, resulting in four. Providing he got a hold, though. And a feature hold. If you don't get a feature hold, the numbers just go back down to zero.

He went to the bar to get change of a tenner. He asked for a fiver and five pound coins – he didn't want the temptation to shove a tenner's worth of coins in. The lassie came back with ten pound coins anyway, she said they never had any fivers. He said that was fine and cracked some joke about the fruit machine. She didn't hear him, and walked away.

He headed back to the fruit machine and stuck in a pound. No hold, no feature hold. Nothing.

Then he stuck in the rest of the tenner, and got nothing.

He went back to the bar and asked for change of a twenty. She asked if he wanted a tenner and ten pound coins. He said no thanks, he wanted twenty pound coins please.

He stuck in the lot, but won two quid back. Then he stuck that in, and got nothing.

He went back to the bar for more change, but noticed he had no cash in his wallet. He asked if they did cash-back, but they didn't. The lassie told him that there was a cash machine next to the toilet, so he headed to that. It charged him £2.95 to use it, so he made it worth his while and took out a hundred.

He went to the bar and bought another pint, getting change of a twenty while he was at it.

He walked over to the machine, put his pint on the top, and filled the slot with five quid before hitting start. One, two, three, four, five quid in. Start.

Nothing.

He picked up his pint to walk away; he wasn't going to fill the machine up with the rest of his money, fuck that. Then he changed his mind and put his pint back down and decided that he'd stick a few more quid in after all. But he'd keep ten of the pound coins in his pocket, he wouldn't spend that. He'd just spend the change from the pint. He stuck it in, and got nothing.

He put in the other ten pound coins, and got nothing from that either.

He walked to the bar to get change of another twenty, then saw a young couple enter the pub. He got change of another twenty, just in case. He got it just in case he headed to the bar after this twenty was done and the couple swooped in and got the jackpot. So he got change of forty. He wasn't planning on shoving in forty, mind you, but better safe than sorry.

He went back to the machine, and shoved in forty.

Nothing.

He headed to the bar to get more change, watching the couple like a hawk. If they tried to swoop in on the machine, he'd make sure he was there first, even if he had to pretend that he still had a credit left. But they didn't swoop in. They were too busy having a laugh.

He was going to ask for sixty pound coins, but saw that he only had forty quid left in his wallet, so he asked for forty. To get that, the lassie at the bar had to go round the back and empty out those wee see-through bags of change. She cracked some joke about the fruit machine. He didn't hear her, and walked away.

With the first pound coin, he got onto the feature, at last. The game asked him to pick higher or lower than a two, on a reel numbered one to twelve. He picked higher.

It came back with a one.

Nothing.

He stuck in the rest of the forty in no time. He might have won something, but it wasn't much, and it went right back in.

When he was finished, he thought about getting more change, but something inside him decided not to bother. He found a seat and looked at the projector screen for a while, where they usually play the football. The projector wasn't on right now, but he looked at it anyway. Looked through it. He was going to ask them to stick something on, but he decided not to bother.

He looked around. That couple were away.

He stood up to leave and noticed that he hadn't finished his pint, so he sat back down, and looked at the fruit machine. Then decided he'd leave anyway.

As he walked past the machine, he checked his pocket. He had a 5p piece. He walked over to the machine. It was 25p a credit, but sometimes you don't stick in exact multiples of 25p, like when he was shoving in all that smash from before. Maybe there was 20p sitting in the machine right now, waiting for another 5p for a credit.

He was just about to stick the 5p in the slot, then stopped.

He would keep that.

He would keep that 5p.

It seemed ludicrous to keep 5p when you've just stuck in almost a hundred and fifty quid, but no, he would keep that. Because it wasn't just five pence. It was a symbol. A symbol of control. And if he could stop himself from putting in that last 5p, then it meant he could also . . .

He put it in.

Nothing.

SENSITIVE PETE

There once was this guy, a sensitive type of guy, called Pete. He was so sensitive that his mates thought it would be hilarious to send him a video of a guy being killed.

Pete didn't like videos like that, he found them to be deeply disturbing. He'd never watched any before, mind you, but the descriptions alone were enough to get him down. Every few weeks, his mates would send a group email linking to the latest video doing the rounds. 'Oh, you've got to see it,' they'd say. 'There's this guy with a saw,' or 'There's this guy that gets shoved in this box,' or 'This guy puts this thing to his head, thinking it isn't plugged in, but what happens is . . .' No, fuck off. Fuck off with that, stop talking. It was almost worse than watching the video itself, he imagined. By not watching it, his imagination would fill in the blanks, it would imagine the sounds, it would imagine the expression on the victim's face, it would imagine the smell. It was almost tempting to have a look, to compare what was in his mind to the video itself, but he never did. He'd read the description, get the shudders and give it a miss. This time, though, they didn't give a description. Not an accurate one, anyway. You know, for a laugh.

They told him it was an advert for a travel company, a cheesy and unintentionally funny promotional video that they all thought he'd like. He'd heard about it but never seen it, so he clicked on the link. But what he got was something else. Before he knew it, screams were blasting from his laptop speakers, as he watched a man go from being alive to being dead.

It was horrific. Pete felt his face go pale. His hands felt cold and sweaty. He felt spaced out. When it was finished, he stood up and looked out the window, at nothing. He chewed the fingernail on his thumb. He put on the kettle to try and carry on as normal, but it was no use. He couldn't get it out of his mind. It was there at the forefront, no matter what he did. It would maybe leave his thoughts for five seconds or so, then it would be back. He went for a walk, he stared at some ducks, he went to the shops and bought a new top, his mum phoned and they talked about how she was getting rid of her microwave because the light inside didn't work any more. And all the time, there was that guy, in Pete's head, getting done in.

So Pete tried something to get that video out of his mind, he decided to do something that maybe went against common sense.

He decided to watch it again.

He thought it would be best to go back and watch it again until it became normal. Maybe the problem was that he was too sensitive. Maybe he needed to watch it over and over until he toughened up. So he did. He watched it over and over, over and over. Ten times, forty times, countless times, until he wasn't that bothered, until he couldn't care less, until he actually started to see the funny side. He went back to one of the old links he'd been sent by his mates, one he'd never clicked. He read the description and remembered his distress at reading it the first time around, but this time he felt nothing. And when he watched the video, he discovered he was all right with that as well.

He liked his new thick skin. He didn't realise how much of a scaredy cat he was before, hiding away, shutting his eyes, not prepared to fully accept what was really going on out there. Living life by half. Half a person. Now he felt complete. He felt strong. The video had helped him cope better with day-to-day life, in a way, with stuff on the news, with family tragedies, terrible stuff, stuff he used to care about, stuff that used to break his heart, and now it didn't. He wasn't a religious man, but there was something almost spiritual about it.

He began watching more, more of that stuff; there were whole sites dedicated to it. It had a profound effect: it brought about a kind of awakening. It reminded him of when he was told Santa didn't exist; it was upsetting, but there was something empowering about knowing the truth. You could almost feel it in your lungs, you could feel it in your mind, that stretch, as you realised that what you thought was real was nothing but a fairy tale. And there it was with each new video, each new horror, that painful but rewarding feeling of being warped.

But eventually the videos weren't enough. They weren't real. They were recordings of something real in the past, but they weren't real, they were rectangular and flat, they weren't here and now and all around. That stretching feeling became more and more rare, it was hard to get. It looked like he'd reached a dead end, and it made him a bit glum. Then one day he saw something that cheered him right up. He saw a guy getting hit by the side mirror of a bus. Pete saw it coming, he could have shouted over to tell the guy to look out, but he chose to just watch instead. An ambulance was called, and Pete looked on, feeling that stretch he hadn't felt in quite some time, as he thought, I did that.

Well, what came next was only a matter of time.

'Barbaric!' said the judge.

Pete had sent his mates a video. It was a good video, it didn't just have one thing in it, it had lots of things, like a compilation album. There was an old man at the top of a flight of concrete steps; just as he was about hold on to the handle and take his first step, a foot came out from behind the camera and kicked him flying. There was a steaming guy sleeping in a doorway, a smart/casual type in his twenties at the end of a night out; a hand came out from behind the camera and pushed a nail into his neck. Then there was this silver-haired businessman with his head in a vice, getting his balls taken off with a can opener. Pete ended it by turning the camera on himself and giving a big thumbs-up and a smile and wave to his mates, which was a mistake, looking back. You would have thought they'd have been all right with it with all the shite they were into. Grassing bastards.

'Barbaric!' said the judge.

Haha. Fuck off, ya prick. Man up.

TOMATO SOUP

Iain held the spoon of tomato soup an inch from his mouth, motionless, as he stared out the cafe window with his jaw on the deck.

Outside, at the other side of the road, was his mum. There she was. They weren't due to meet for lunch or anything; she had no idea he was in there staring out at her. If she did, he was quite sure she wouldn't be doing what she was doing.

She was kissing a guy.

Some of the soup on the spoon dripped down into the bowl below, splashing one or two drops onto Iain's T-shirt. He didn't notice. His mum was kissing some guy.

He felt like chapping the window to get her to stop, the way a primary school teacher might chap on a window with keys to stop one of the children flashing their genitals. But he didn't. As much as he didn't want to see his mum like that, he didn't want to see his mum seeing him seeing her like that. But she'd find out eventually. She'd find out that he'd found out, because he'd have to tell his dad. He'd have to. 'Dad,' he'd say. 'Know how you and Mum stopped shagging years ago? She's still at it, mate. She's still at it.'

She squeezed the guy's arse. Iain lowered his spoon into the bowl and pushed it away.

They stopped kissing for a moment, only to adjust their heads and get fired right back into each other once again. Iain could almost see the guy's face now, but not quite, he couldn't get a good, clear look. However, he did get a good, clear look at the semi that was bulging through the guy's middle-age trousers. He saw that all right. He was surprised at how little he was shocked by it. Surprised and concerned. Concerned at what it meant for his mental health, as he had clearly become warped. He looked away. He reckoned that when he got round to telling his dad, he'd maybe leave this bit out. Dad needed to know the truth, but he didn't need to be tortured with it.

Iain looked back at the pair of them. They'd turned slightly, and now Iain could get a good, clear look at the guy's face.

His heart sank.

No. No, it can't be.

Iain leaned his elbows against the table, closed his eyes and gently put his palms against his face. He wouldn't be telling his dad after all. Not now. If the guy had been a stranger, aye, but not now.

It was bad. Pretty bad.

It was Dad.

Mum was with Dad.

The cafe owner walked over to Iain, the guy at the window, the one who'd been staring into his soup for the last fifteen minutes. 'Is everything OK?' she asked, looking at the soup. She'd made it herself.

'It's revolting,' he whispered. 'Revolting.'

Suit yourself.

CRAP FILMS

I've got a mate, he's a bit of a film buff. He's got it in his Twitter bio: 'Film buff'. He's the sort of guy that refers to films like *Rear Window* simply as *Window*. I remember asking him why he did that, and he said that if you're into films as much as he is and discuss them as much as he does, then it just makes more sense, it saves a lot of time. I told him that I understood why he sometimes shortened *One Flew Over the Cuckoo's Nest* to *One Flew*, even though it's not something I'd do myself, but shortening *Rear Window* to *Window*? You're only losing a syllable. I remember saying that to him online one night, I said, 'Are you sure you don't just do it to sound clever?' but he never replied. Have a sense of humour, mate, fuck's sake.

Anyway, I recommended a film to him, because I'm a bit of a film buff myself. Not enough to stick 'Film buff' in my bio, mind you, I don't take myself that seriously, but I know a good film when I see one. And this one I recommended was good. It was Danish. I told him about it, and a few days later I asked him what he thought. He said he thought it was crap.

That was the word he used: 'Crap'.

I told him I thought that was quite blunt, telling me one of my favourite films was crap, and I laughed. I laughed to pretend that it didn't bother me, but it did. I think what he said was actually out of order, it was just fucking rude. He said he didn't mean to offend me; I told him that I wasn't offended, it was only a film, haha. He said that it's not as if I made it or anything; I told him I knew I never made it, I wasn't claiming I made it, just drop it, it isn't a big deal. But I did say to him that to tell me one of my favourite films is crap, all matter-of-fact like that, some people would find that offensive. He said he didn't say it was crap, he said he just thought it was crap, on a subjective and personal level. He said it wasn't like he was saying I liked crap things. I said that's exactly what he was saying. He said it wasn't, it was just that he thought it was crap himself, that's all. I personally don't see the difference, but I told him again to just drop it, it isn't a big deal. Haha.

So he dropped it. But then I told him to recommend a film to me. 'On you go.' He said he didn't want to. I said, 'No, go on, recommend your favourite film to me. Go.' So he did. He recommended a few, and I told him no, I wanted his favourite favourite. Step into the spotlight, mate, and recommend your all-time favourite. He said it was really hard to pick an all-time favourite, and I laughed. Calls himself a film buff yet he struggles to pick his favourite film. But eventually he picked one. Eventually we got one out of him. Hallelujah.

So I watched it, and it was good. I liked it. I really liked it. I'd say it's one of my top ten films, in fact. The sort of film you like even more as time goes on, long after you've watched it. It just keeps popping into your head now and again. Brilliant film. Anyway, after I watched it, I sent him a message, and told him it was crap.

He said, well, that's my opinion and that I'm entitled to my opinion, just like he was entitled to his. I said no, it wasn't my opinion, it was a fact, his film was crap – 'Sorry to break it to you, mate, but it was.' He told me again that I was entitled to my opinion, but that a lot of people disagreed with that opinion. I told him, that they were wrong as well then. He said, 'Wrong?' and asked me if I was saying he was wrong to like that film, if having that film as his favourite was, in the eyes of the universe, wrong. I said, 'Maybe.'

He said he needed to go, but I told him to wait because it was my turn to recommend a film. He told me he didn't want to get into all this any more. I asked him what he meant, get into what? I was only wanting to recommend a fucking film, he needed to seriously lighten up. He said all right and that I was to message him when I thought of one, but I already had one in mind. I told him what the film was, and he said he'd watch it but I wasn't to get offended if he thought it was crap. I told him that I'm not that easily offended, mate, I'm a big boy. And anyway, I won't mind if he thinks it's crap, because I think it's crap as well.

He asked me to repeat what I said. Did I just recommend a film to him that I thought was crap? I said, 'That's right.' He asked me why. I told him that although I thought it was crap, I reckoned it would be right up his street. Because that's the sort of thing he likes: crap. He told me he wasn't going to watch it, and he didn't like the way this whole film thing had 'soured' things between us. I laughed it off and told him that I didn't sense any sourness, if there was any then it was coming from his end, and that I was sorry to hear that. I told him to just watch the film. He said, 'No,' then went offline.

But I know that he will. And I know what he's going to say. He's going to say that he liked it, and that I only think it's crap because I don't get it. But then I'll have him, because then I'll tell him the truth. And the truth is that I don't think it's crap. It's actually one of my favourite films. The look on his face when I tell him that, when he realises what he's done, when he realises that he's effectively admitted that I do know my stuff, despite me not having 'Film buff' in my bio, despite me not having studied films in college when I was too busy working, mate, despite me not being one of his new intellectual crowd that he's so fond of tweeting pictures of these days.

I cannot fucking wait to see the look on his face. I haven't seen him in a while, though. A good few months. He said he's snowed under with work.

'Work', haha.

What does he know about work?

THE WALLET

There once was a man who found a wallet. He found a wallet on a train, a wallet that wasn't his, and he kept it. What a dick.

This wallet was made of black leather with a light grey elasticated band, and on the band was a wee red label that was half hanging off due to wear and tear. In fact, it was a bit like my own wallet. The one that I lost. But this isn't about my wallet, this is another wallet. This is just a story.

Now, the wallet itself was worthless. Like I said, it had suffered from a good bit of wear and tear over the years, it was even a bit stinking. It was what was inside the wallet that was the most costly. It wasn't losing the cash that was costly, I don't think there was that much cash in it. It was the cards, the bank cards. Losing the cards was costly, in terms of time. The poor guy who lost the wallet had to phone up and get all the fucking cards cancelled, and you know what that can be like, those call centres. The waiting.

Having to prove that you are who you say you are, then getting put through to somebody else, then having to explain everything again to them, then getting cut off, then having to start from the beginning with somebody else. Then eventually you have to actually just go into the branch in person, like it's the fucking Seventies.

Sorry, did I say that the poor guy 'lost' the wallet? That's not quite right, is it? It was stolen, because to take a lost wallet and then not hand it in, that's theft. Look it up. You can't just pick things up that don't belong to you just because the person that owns it isn't there at that time. That's theft. You may as well have took it right out of my fucking pocket, mate.

Sorry, not 'my' pocket, I mean the poor bastard who lost the wallet. Because, remember, this isn't about my wallet, this is another wallet, this is just a story. Any similarities between anybody in this story and any real person living or dead are purely coincidental, etc., etc. You've got to say that in case you get sued. But I don't need to say it anyway, because it's just a story. The guy who took the wallet, he's not real, completely fictitious. And now that I've said that, let me say this . . .

I want this guy dead.

Or woman. Could be a woman. But probably a guy. And I want him dead.

In the story, I mean. It's important for me to say again, for legal reasons, that this is just a story, in case I get done for encouraging somebody to do me a big, big favour and kill this guy for me.

Now, back to the story. Will anybody bring this chap to justice? Who will be my hero?

Maybe somebody in the story finds out that a guy they know had recently come by a wallet. Maybe the guy they know is a colleague or a friend or a family member, boasting about finding a wallet on a train, a black leather wallet with a light grey elasticated band with a wee red label on it that's half hanging off. Maybe the guy mentioned something about trying to guess the PIN at cash machines in the Finnieston, Partick and Hyndland areas of Glasgow, according to what the banks said. The banks in the story.

And maybe that person in the story, the one who discovers the villain, our hero, is a decent person and they feel outraged, and feel angry, and want to do something to redress the balance. So maybe they do something to bring harm to the thief. Maybe if they work with the thief, they could serve him a cup of tea, with some bleach in it. Or maybe if they live with the thief and the thief is fitting a new light or whatever, our hero could tell him that the electricity is safely switched off, when it isn't. Something like that. It's really up to them.

It's really up to you.

It's really up to you, because this is one of those stories that leave the ending up to your imagination. I'm going to leave the ending open. I'm going to leave it up to you.

I hope you give it the happy ending it deserves.

THE BLANK BUTTON

Charlie was about to get the attention of the waitress, before noticing the wee device on the table, the one with the buttons. One button was for the bill, one was for service and one was blank. He pressed the one for service, and sure enough, a minute later, over walked a waitress asking how she could help. Charlie asked for one last cup of tea and that was that. When he was finished, he pressed the button for the bill, and a minute later, over came the waitress with the bill in her hand.

As he was getting on his jacket, ready to leave, he had a look at the device again. He had a look at the button. You know which one. The one with nothing on it, the blank one. He wondered what it was for. He was going to press it before walking away, but he was forty years old, that would be juvenile. One of the waiters walked by, and Charlie felt like stopping him to ask what the button did, but the guy looked like a bit of a grumpy sort so Charlie didn't bother.

Charlie pushed out his seat to stand and head for the door, but before he left he had one more look at that button. What did it do? It wouldn't hurt to press it now – he was just about to leave; if something embarrassing happened it would be all right, he was heading for the door. So he pressed it, and started walking slowly towards the way out, looking around, looking behind, curious to see what would happen. But nothing did. Not right away.

As Charlie got to the door, he saw the grumpy waiter walk over to the table where Charlie was sitting. When the waiter saw that nobody was there, he looked around, puzzled, before looking at Charlie. Charlie was about to turn to walk out, but he saw the waiter walk towards him, waving for him to stop. Charlie wanted to make a run for it, but he didn't want to look like a teenager, so he stood his ground. Besides, he wanted to know what the button was for. It was blank, so why did the waiter come over?

The waiter came over to Charlie, and spoke quietly. He asked Charlie if he pressed that button. Charlie denied it, thinking that he could get away with saying that he must have pressed it accidentally, if this all turned serious. The waiter apologised, then turned to walk away. Charlie stopped him by saying aye, he did do it. The waiter turned back towards Charlie and asked him why. Why did he do it? Charlie replied with another question: what's it for? Why is it blank? The waiter said it was blank because it used to be a button for ordering a drink, but seeing as there was already a button to get service, it only caused confusion, so they rubbed it out. But that was beside the point: the waiter wanted to know why Charlie pressed it. He took a step towards Charlie, looked over his shoulders, then whispered the question.

'Why?'

Charlie felt uncomfortable, he didn't know what was going on here really. He answered the question. He was curious, that's all. Just curious. The waiter asked him if he was a curious type of person, and Charlie said yes. The waiter said that was good, because he was the curious type as well.

Charlie pointed out that he wasn't gay. He wasn't sure if that's what this was, but he wasn't, no offence. The waiter said he wasn't either. He just meant he was like Charlie. Curious. Curious about what's out there. He was into trying new things. Unknown things. Nothing illegal, of course. Just stuff that's a bit off the beaten path.

Charlie told the waiter that that sounded interesting.

I saw them on the news the other day.

They got twenty years apiece.

SMALL PRINT

He was standing at the platform in the underground, waiting for his train. He couldn't get Twitter down here, so he had a look around. He glanced to the left and saw folk staring into space. He glanced to the right and saw a newspaper on a seat that he couldn't be bothered reading. So he just glanced ahead at the posters on the wall at the other side of the track. It certainly was a good place to advertise: there was nowhere else to look.

One of the posters was for hair straighteners. Another was for holiday homes or something like that. But this one straight ahead was quite intriguing. It was intriguing because it wasn't that obvious what it was for. All it was was a giant '0%' and nothing more. It didn't say if it was 0 per cent finance, or if it was the percentage of people who said they were unhappy with whatever product it was, if it was a product at all. It was just this big '0%'.

Oh, and some small print at the bottom.

The man leaned his head forward a bit to read the small print, to see what these folk were trying to sell him, but he couldn't see. He took a tiny step forward, leaned out again, but still, the words were just a bit too small. So he left it.

He waited a bit longer, waited for his train, and looked around once again. The people, the newspaper, then that poster again with the small print. He heard the train coming, finally.

As people started to nudge their way to the front, he stepped closer to the edge, and glanced at the poster once more, at the small print in particular. It was almost in focus, but not quite. He quite fancied seeing what the fuck the small print said before he got on the train; he knew it would bug him if he didn't.

He stepped even closer to the edge, and leaned forward, putting his head out just that wee bit more, then just a wee bit more than that. Then he fell onto the fucking track.

A few folk shouted to him, thinking he was trying to top himself. But he stood up quickly and said he was fine. A few helping hands shot out, offering to pull him back up to the platform, and he was just about to grab one. But now that he was down there . . .

You know, now that he was down there . . .

He turned towards the poster. It was still a bit out of focus. He walked towards it; people shouted at him to get back onto the fucking platform, the train's coming. He could see one guy ready to jump down, so he told the guy to fuck off, he's fine, he'll jump up as soon as he's seen this poster. It would be a shame not to, now that he was down there, now that he was so close.

He looked at the small print and noticed that one of the reasons it appeared out of focus was that it was covered in a thin layer of grime from the trains. He wiped it, and started to read what it said underneath.

It was just some shite about 0 per cent finance on something, and how you'd have to start paying within a certain time otherwise it would go up to some other APR, a lot of mumbo jumbo. The reason why there was so little info about the product was because it was a kind of teaser campaign to get dafties like our man interested before revealing the product a week or so later, but they had to put in the mumbo jumbo for legal reasons.

He never found that out, though, he never got further than two or three words in, because he got hit by the fucking train, didn't he? As he did, one of the commuters turned to a woman next to him. And do you know what he said?

He said, 'Now there's one case where you definitely shouldn't read the small print!'

What an absolute cracker!

Unfortunately, she didn't quite catch it. She was in shock.

A man had just lost his life.

ME AGAIN

You're walking through a shop, a clothes shop, looking down at some clothes on the racks. You look up, and you make eye contact with another person. You're quite sure they were looking at you first, but you're willing to accept that you both looked at each other at near enough the same time. But they look at you like you're the one that looked first, like you were caught staring, like you're the bad one. They dump the clothes they were thinking of getting and walk away. Fucking oddball.

An hour or so later, you go for lunch. You're in a restaurant miles away from that shop, nowhere near it. You sit down at a table, look around: who's at the table next you? That person.

They're not looking at you, not yet anyway, but you're looking at them, thinking about how much of a coincidence that is, and also how it's a bit weird. But it's not half as weird as how you feel when they look up and catch you staring at them. It's you again. You that was looking at them in the shop earlier today, a shop that's miles away, and now here you are in this restaurant sitting at the next table, staring at them. You give a wee smile and open your mouth to comment on how much of a coincidence it is, but you get as far as a croak sound before they bury their nose in the menu. You shrug your shoulders and look back to your table. You pick up a menu and act normal, to try and make it not look like a big deal, that these things happen. But then you over-hear the waiter ask the person if they'd like to order and they say no, they've changed their mind. You hear them get up and head towards the door. Fucking hell. Not only that, they take the long way around to the door so as to not have to brush past you. You look down at your menu, shake your head and look up to see them walking past the window outside, staring at you. When they see you staring back, they get a wee fright, like you've just proven to them that you're a mad staring weirdo, that you are a bad one, even though it was them that fucking stared first. It was them that fucking stared first!

An hour later, you're walking through the park. You get to a wee secluded bit, a wee path that not many people walk through. And surprise surprise, who's this walking towards you in the distance? It's them.

You couldn't make this up.

But they haven't seen you yet, and you just know that you can't do this again, you just can't. So you walk off the path and hide behind a tree. That's right, you hide behind a tree. You've done nothing wrong, yet you hide behind a fucking tree. It'll just be until they walk past, then you'll go back on the path and get the fuck out of there and hopefully never bump into them again. You'll emigrate if you have to.

As you hear them walk past, you turn your head slightly to see if they're gone, and you step on a twig. The twig snaps. The person stops and turns.

And sees you staring at them from behind a tree.

They run like fuck, and start shouting. What the fuck are they doing? You run after them to explain, there's no way you can let it get out that you're some kind of stalker, you need to explain and get them to see the funny side of all this. You almost catch up, you almost grab their shoulder, but then they stop in their tracks, turn around and belt you in the face. You're bleeding.

You could say that was fair, you could say it was self-defence and then use this moment to try to explain, but why are you the one who has to do all the explaining? You're not the one in the wrong here; you're both as wrong as each other. They stared at you first, have we forgotten that? No. So you belt them back, just to assert the fact you are both equals here.

Crack. You break their nose. You didn't mean that.

They make a run for the trees, terrified, and you chase after them. After losing them briefly, they come out of nowhere with a boulder and smack it over your head. You hit the deck. You reckon that's it, you reckon they'll run away and that it'll be them that's emigrating. But then they lift the boulder again. They're going to finish you off. You boot their shin and they drop the boulder on their foot. You boot them in the belly and down they go. They reach for the boulder, winded, but you get there first. You pick the boulder and lift it high and you bring it down on their skull.

You've killed them.

You can see the brain. You've killed them. Jesus Christ, you killed them.

So it turns out they were right about you.

You are a bad one.

Turns out they were right about you all along.

THE PIGEON DANCE

It was one of those religious debates. It was quite a big deal, this one. It was all being professionally shot and streamed live onto YouTube, with tons of viewers leaving tons of comments in the comments bit below. On the stage were three people. In the middle was the chairwoman, a familiar face from the news, brought in for her experience in keeping order between her guests on the telly and making sure questions were answered. Beside her were the two opponents. To the left was the guy on the side of religion, a pretty high-up religious figure himself, not as high as the Pope, but halfway there. On the right was the guy against religion, the atheist. And before them all was the audience, who had turned up to watch this pair arguing like fuck for an hour.

They'd been at it for about forty-five minutes, arguing mainly about creationism, intelligent design, how things came about and why they do the things they do. With fifteen minutes left, the chairwoman decided it was time now to take some questions from the crowd. And what a crowd it was, it was packed, because the atheist on stage wasn't just any old atheist. It was none other than renowned biologist Richard Dawkins himself. Richard smiled as he turned to face everybody, ready for whatever questions they were about to throw. He was feeling confident, he was feeling at ease – things had gone quite well for him. Unlike the other guy. Despite Richard's opponent being this religious big shot, despite him being one of these guys you'd see on the telly at Christmas or at a state funeral, in a big cathedral, dressed in robes and a hat, commanding all this respect and reverence from politicians and royalty, despite all that, Richard had made him look like a right wee fanny.

The chairwoman asked the audience for a question. A few people stuck their hands up; the chairwoman looked around, then picked one from down the front. The lady in the white top. She stood up and got handed a mic. It was a question for Dawkins. If there was no God, she asked, how could he account for so and so? It was a good question; a few of the religious folk in the audience looked to Richard to see how he'd respond. They kind of wished that they'd asked it themselves, until Dawkins tore her to shreds, then they were kind of glad that they hadn't. She sat back down, her face red, and handed back the mic.

The hands went up again. The chairwoman decided to go for somebody up the back. The man with the chequered shirt. It was a question for the religious guy. Some religious people, he said, take the story of Creation in Genesis literally, but other religious people, within that very same religion, don't. How can we account for such and such? The religious guy thanked the man for the question, and said that it was a very interesting question, and an important question, and one that he would like to now answer. He managed to get about halfway into his response before Richard jumped in at something that didn't make sense. The atheists laughed and applauded. The chairwoman asked Richard not to interrupt, but the damage was done, the religious guy looked like a total fucking dope once again.

And then another question from the audience. And another. Point after point to Dawkins. Most of them were easy wins, but some of them not so easy. There were quite a few religious scientists in the audience who spoke with very big words, most of which went right over the head of the rest of the audience and the viewers on YouTube. But Richard knew what they meant, and fired back one or two big words of his own. The religious scientists sat down, and stayed down. After that, no more hands went up.

It had been a very successful afternoon for Richard. He was glad they were filming it, he was glad it was live, it had an edgy feel to it. Oh, he was always on the ball whether it was live or not, or even if it wasn't being filmed at all, but there was something he enjoyed about being watched by anonymous eyes around the world, willing him to trip up or get caught out, and being disappointed. The stakes were high. It was exhilarating. He glanced over to one of the cameramen, and saw him yawn and look at his watch. It was healthy to see that to some people this didn't matter a jot. It put things into perspective. Richard wondered if it was nearly time to go. The chairwoman read his mind.

'Well, I think it's just about time to go,' she said. 'I'd like to thank— Oh, we have one more question.' Richard looked towards the audience. 'The man in the grey T-shirt.' She pointed towards the centre of the crowd, where a man had his hand raised. He was handed the mic, then he stood up. Richard couldn't help smiling. He didn't mean to judge, but the guy was a slob. He had a big baggy faded grey T-shirt, tight around the midriff, with crumbs and a smudge of sauce on the chest. And he looked like his fingers smelled of chips.

'I've got a question for Richard Dawkin,' said the man. He looked in his thirties, but his voice was high like a twelve-year-old's, like it hadn't broke yet. Richard had to stop himself from laughing. It was the voice, the state of that T-shirt, plus the fact the guy had called him Richard Dawkin, not Dawkins. It made Richard happy; this would be a nice easy one before he got out of there. A bit of comedy. He'd be gentle with him, he'd end on a laugh. These debates made him come across as quite serious, quite angry, quite self-righteous. He'd never apologise for being right, but he was aware he sometimes appeared arrogant and uncompromising. Some said he was every bit as fanatical as a religious zealot. A bit of comedy here would be the perfect way to end this, to leave on a high note. A wee giggle to relax everybody's shoulders.

'Aye, what it is is,' said the slob, 'I'll tell you what it is. You know pigeons?'

Richard didn't respond at first, thinking the slob wasn't actually wanting an answer, but he was. 'Yes,' said Richard, which got a wee titter from the audience.

'You know how you sometimes see the guy pigeon doing that wee dance around the lassie pigeon, when it wants a ride?'

A few audience members laughed out loud. The slob didn't get what was funny. Quite a character, this one. Richard tried to keep a straight face. 'Yes, if I understand your meaning.'

'Well, I suppose my question is . . . what's that all about?'

Some members of the audience put their hands over their faces and shook their heads, even the religious ones. Richard felt himself about to laugh again, but he thought he better not, because it might come out later that the guy has something wrong with him. Neither should he palm the guy off with a jokey response, because that might seem patronising, like a jokey response is all a joke of a man deserves. No, he'd give a serious answer like any other, he couldn't go wrong there.

'Well,' began Dawkins, before pausing for thought.

He paused for quite a while. The audience was quiet.

What was that all about? The pigeon dance. He'd seen it before, it was quite a funny thing to watch, but he'd never given it much thought, other than filing it under one of many mating rituals that many other creatures perform instinctively. He could reply simply with that and get out of here, but it seemed too simplistic. That dance, that way the male would trot after the female, before doing a wee turn on the spot, bobbing its head down as it turned, without ever being taught. It was almost like seeing a toddler doing the dance from *Thriller* without ever having seen the video. Quite mind-boggling, really.

'Well,' said Dawkins again. 'Um . . .' The audience members with their heads in their hands began to look towards him. He could see the brows of the smiling atheists begin to furrow. It was a most peculiar sight for them. A most peculiar sight.

But really, that dance. What was that all about? If there really was no creator, no God, then where was that dance stored? In the brain, in the blood, in the DNA? Yes. But where? How was the choreography of the pigeon dance written in genetic code? How do you write in genetic code, in that tiny brain, the instruction that this bird must do this dance, it must turn on the spot every so often, not too often, just often enough, and it must bob its head low when it does so? How was that written? How did those genetic instructions look under the microscope? He wasn't sure exactly, but they were there all right, they had to be. But then didn't that mean it would be possible, in theory, to genetically programme a human to have the instinct to do the dance from *Thriller*, right out the womb, right from the word go, including that human's descendants? Did he think he could stand here on stage and make that claim without being laughed out the building? Then why did he think he could make roughly the same claim for the pigeon dance? What would he say? Where was he going with this?

'The, um . . .' His voice sounded weak, his throat felt tight. It felt like the room had got smaller, like the walls had closed in a touch, bringing everybody inside just that wee bit closer to him. He closed his eyes to think, but had to open them right away – it made him feel like he was in a fucking coffin. He suddenly wished this wasn't being broadcast live after all. He glanced over to the cameraman to see that yawning face, to get some perspective, to remind him that all this mattered not one jot, but the cameraman was alert, his brow furrowed like the rest. Even he, a guy who took no interest in this religious atheism bollocks, knew that the smart-arse guy on stage was in trouble.

Richard was about to go for a jokey response after all, he almost wanted to say that it was easily the most ridiculous question he had ever been asked; he knew it was a risky thing to say to somebody who potentially had something wrong with them, but he was getting desperate. Fortunately, the chairwoman stepped in. Richard looked down to the notepad on his lap, to hide his face from the audience. He hoped she'd now be bringing the event to an end. But no.

'Correct me if I'm wrong, sir,' said the chairwoman to

the slob, 'but you're asking where exactly does that knowledge come from?'

'Aye,' said the man. 'That wee dance that he does. The pigeon. Like this.' Richard didn't look up. He couldn't bring himself to raise his head to that crowd, and to the cameras; his face felt chained to the floor. He didn't need to look anyway, he could tell what the slob was doing just by the sounds. He could hear his feet tapping against the lino floor, trotting away like a pigeon. He could tell when the guy was turning on the spot, because he could hear the guy's trainers squeak and hear his arse bump his seat out the way. It would normally be a cause for hilarity, a guy like that doing a thing like that right in the middle of an event like that, especially because the guy's big arse and wee head sort of made him look like a pigeon anyway, but the place was silent, except for the guy.

Dawkins glanced up without moving his head, towards the faces of his enemies in the crowd. All eyes on him. He glanced to his opponent on the stage. Was that a faint smile on his face? Dawkins opened his mouth to speak, but nothing came out. It was as if somebody had a Richard Dawkins voodoo doll and was holding it underwater. He couldn't breathe. He was choking. He had the fucking fear.

'Richard,' said the chairwoman, 'would you like to—'

He stood up and ran. He ran off the stage, and opened a door and ran through. It was a cupboard. He ran back out, opened another door then ran down the corridor and out the foyer and down the street. He didn't stop running for ten minutes.

The next day, he tweeted a link to a statement saying he had suffered a panic attack due to his exhaustive schedule. Nobody believed him, the video was already everywhere. He was finished.

He wasn't seen again.

But I saw him, the other day.

He was in the park, feeding the birds. Pigeons, funnily enough. He was wearing pyjamas and dirty socks.

I saw him watch one pigeon in particular, as it did a wee dance around another. He looked deep in thought, like he was staring at a crossword clue, trying to work out what it meant. Then an expression crept across his face, one of understanding. A eureka moment!

But then he shook his head as he seemed to realise a flaw in his thinking. He had another eureka moment, which went as quickly as it came. Then again. And then he lost his rag.

He chucked his bag of bread at the pigeons and gave chase, shouting stuff. Chased them over to the pond, then jumped in. He ran after them, until the water was up to his waist, then up to his neck, until he was out his depth. Then he started to drown.

A few of us looked at each other, wondering if we should help, but we decided against it.

We thought it was best.

LAPTOP

There once was a laptop that wouldn't start up. It used to be fine, years ago, nice and fast, no problems, the occasional crash but that was to be expected with computers. Then, for whatever reason, the crashes got a bit more frequent, and happened for no apparent reason. It wasn't like the laptop was being pushed to the limits, very little was asked of it, yet it crashed. It just seemed to crash whenever it felt like it, and that gave its owner a bit of a headache. Sometimes the crashes would be no more than a minor inconvenience, crashing while reading a blog or watching a video, nothing to tear your hair out over. Other times it would crash in the middle of filling out a form, which was a bit more annoying, because it would mean having to reboot, go back to the website and fill in the form from the beginning, with no guarantee that it wouldn't crash again. Still, it wasn't the end of the world. He could cope. Until now. Until this most recent crash. This was a biggy. Now the thing wouldn't start up. It would look like it was about to start up, then he'd get the blue screen thing and get no further. And that seriously put him out.

It was really important the laptop started up, because these days the owner wasn't just using it to watch stuff on YouTube or whatever, he couldn't just shrug it off and pull out his phone instead. At the moment he was using it to write a book. Just a collection of daft wee stories, but it was still a book, it was still important. Not only that, he had nearly finished. The whole book was on this laptop, the deadline was approaching and if the laptop wouldn't switch on any more then quite frankly it was game over. It was game over.

He tried switching the laptop on again, but again it didn't start. Blue screen. It'd happened before, the blue screen at start-up, but then he'd try again and it would work. But now, nope. Blue screen, time and time again. It was just not fucking starting. So he picked up his pen and began to write. No, he hadn't decided to write the book from scratch, it wasn't a story he was writing. It was a threat. A threat to the laptop. A promise. And his promise was this.

The next time he switched on that laptop, it had better start. It had better fucking start, or it was going in the bin. It was getting kicked the fuck out of, its keys were getting torn off, its screen was getting scratched with a fork and its electronics were getting pished on, then it was going in the bin. It was getting fucking melted, then it was going in the bin. This was its last chance. Its final chance. It wasn't a bluff: he could walk out the door and buy a new laptop that very day. Nothing stopping him. But he thought he'd give the laptop just one last chance. Him and the laptop went way back, after all.

He switched on the laptop.

It worked.

Wise move.

RENNIE

My mate Rennie shags his granda.